GIRL
WITHOUT
SKIN

CONNIE RAMSAY BOTT

To Gwen
with warm wishes,

Connie

INDEPENDENT INNOVATIVE INTERNATIONAL

Published by Cinnamon Press
Meirion House, Tanygrisiau
Blaenau Ffestiniog, Gwynedd LL41 3SU
www.cinnamonpress.com
The right of Connie Ramsay Bott to be identified as author of this work has been asserted by her in accordance with the Copyright, Designs and Patent Act, 1988. © 2017 Connie Ramsay Bott. ISBN 978-1-910836-74-3 British Library Cataloguing in Publication Data. A CIP record for this book can be obtained from the British Library.
Designed and typeset in Garamond by Cinnamon Press. Cover design by Adam Craig © Adam Craig.
Cinnamon Press is represented by Inpress and by the Welsh Books Council in Wales. Printed in Poland.
The publisher gratefully acknowledges the support of the Welsh Books Council.

Acknowledgements

I came to fiction writing well into adulthood. I wasn't sure anything I wrote would be worth reading, so to anyone and everyone early on who encouraged and inspired me, thank you. I greatly appreciate the editing advice and camaraderie of the members of Inktank writing group. Thanks to fellow American Kathy Newitt for helping me to keep it real, and to Judy Meier for believing in me. My special thanks go to Cathy Whittaker for giving me the confidence to make writing such a huge part of my life. I am indebted to Jan Fortune, my mentor and editor, for all her help and enthusiasm.

Thanks also the editors of magazines and anthologies where some of these stories were originally published: 'Fire and Blood', *Raw Edge Magazine*; 'Grandma Says', *The Magazine* (anthology) published by Warwick University; 'A Million Miles from Cecile', *Creative Identity* (anthology); 'Watching Robert Duffin', Baker Prize winning story, published by *Northwords Now* (issue 26 Spring 2014) and *Words from an Island*, anthology published by The Skye Reading Room; 'Brothers', *Ariadne's Thread* anthology.

GIRL WITHOUT SKIN

Island
Autumn 1965

'Oh, for God's sake, Spanky. Don't get that hurt look. I only give nicknames to my special friends,' Howard says. I wish he'd just call me Vincent. 'Here,' he says. 'Have a cigarette.'

I shake my head. He stares into my eyes until I have to look away. I gaze over his shoulder across the choppy water to the big island. It's a yellow-green blur from here.

'Come on. Are you worried about your momma smelling them on you? The wind on the lake will blow the smell away. Suit yourself, momma's boy.'

Momma's boy. Momma's good little boy is such a help: he keeps the stuff in his room tidy, he peels the potatoes for dinner and washes the dishes afterwards, he listens when she talks about what a horrible person Dad is, and how they're better off without him. He never disagrees with her, because that's one of the things that makes her cry.

I take one of Howard's cigarettes and he tries to light it for me.

'You're supposed to inhale while I hold the match to it. Breathe in. That's right.'

The thing feels clumsy in my hand and I don't like the taste in my mouth. I let it dangle at my side so that it starts to slowly burn away.

Howard's house is a hundred yards up the beach. It's twice as big as ours, and it's made of wood that's never been painted. My mom says we're lucky to have our little brick house. She says Howard's house is a disgrace, and it ought to be condemned. She says Howard's mother is a disgrace. He's fourteen, and he has five little brothers and sisters. Mom says they all have different fathers, but I don't see how she knows that. When a man comes to visit Howard's mom, and they sit out on the dock drinking beers, mom says it's shameful. 'A shameful woman,' she calls her.

At least Howard's mom knows how to be happy.

'We've got another hour or more of daylight,' Howard says. 'Ten minutes to row out to the island, ten minutes back. We've got plenty of time.'

I think it'll be at least twenty minutes each way, but it's not worth arguing. Most of the leaves have blown off the trees, but Howard hasn't put his rowboat away for the winter. He's in no hurry. He says last year he left it out till the first snow came, and the lake was starting to freeze around it.

Mom says I'm not allowed to hang around with Howard. She says a fourteen year old has no business 'seeking out' an eleven year old. I'm to steer clear of him. This whole place is dead since the summer people went home. Mom is either at work or at home being miserable.

But Howard is interesting, and he did that amazing thing to the wild cat. I didn't know it was wild. Howard said we should try to catch it, to see how friendly it was. When we cornered it behind his house, and I tried to pick it up, the thing lashed out at me and scratched me right through my tee shirt. I had three slashes across my chest, and scratches on my arms. Howard grabbed it by the tail and carried it to the dock. He marched out to the end, the cat yowling and spitting, and dropped it head first into the lake. It swam to shore, and when it got out it was just this skinny thing. I've never seen a cat run so fast.

Howard said, 'I don't think we'll be seeing *him* again,' like he'd just solved some big problem. We laughed and laughed. I had to throw the tee shirt away so Mom didn't see the blood and rips, and I kept the scratches hidden. She noticed one on my hand, but I told her I got it pulling the Frisbee out of a bush.

'I just have to dash in and get something from my bedroom,' Howard says.

It's really strange at Howard's house. There's always so much going on. He shouts at his brothers and sisters, and makes them wait on him and me, and when his mom comes home he's nice as pie, and she doesn't believe them when they tell on him. Once I heard him tell Bobby, the littlest one, that if he didn't stop being a pest, he was going to take him out to the big island and leave him there. Bobby would never be able to swim to shore; it's too far.

I've never been to the island. Mom says it's full of rats and snakes, and I have no business going there. Howard says the island is neat. That's funny, really, because it's surely the opposite of neat, with trees and bushes growing wild. I wouldn't say anything, though, because you don't laugh at Howard. He's going to show me some exciting stuff he has buried there. I told him I didn't want to go, but he got mad, and said I'd better do what he said. Then he said he was just kidding. I don't know how it all got turned around, but I agreed to go.

The cigarette is burned half way down, and I toss it into the dirty foam at the shoreline. I rub my fingers with the wet sand and rinse them off in the lake to try to get rid of the smell. There's lake weed and a few dead fish washed up here and there. The water is steely grey, except for the little whitecaps. Howard comes out of his house carrying a bag with things rattling in it, like metal on metal.

'You row there, Spanky, and I'll row back,' Howard says. He pushes the boat off shore and steps over my seat, with his hand on my head for balance. He sits on the back seat facing me, his hair blowing away from his pimply forehead. Already I know that he's not going to do any rowing, but I don't say anything.

He just has a cloth coat on. He must be freezing, sitting on the aluminum seat while the wind howls around us. And I'm getting hot and sweaty, rowing on the choppy lake in my heavy jacket.

I think the stuff buried must be pictures of naked women. He thinks I've never seen that sort of thing, but I have. One time at my last school, before we moved out of Dad's house, I was in the library with Neil. We were looking at the art books, because a lot of old paintings have women with no clothes on. Sometimes they have parts of themselves covered with flimsy cloth that you can see right through. Sometimes their eyes lock on you, like they know you're looking at them, even though they're only paintings. The librarian came over and saw what we were looking at, and we thought we were in trouble, but she said, 'Those artists were very good at getting the flesh tones just right, don't you think?' Somehow, she made me feel more grown up.

It's taken even longer than I thought it would to row over. The daylight is already going. I can't see how I'll get back before my mom gets home from work. We find a place to pull the boat ashore, and Howard leads me to a grassy patch between two pine trees a little way inland. He takes a little shovel and a bent enamel plate out of his bag. He hands me the plate, and we start digging in a bare spot.

'It's not buried very deep. Won't take a second.'

It's odd. A minute ago I didn't want to be here, but now I want to see what's in the box—this 'treasure' of Howard's. He's right. We shift the sandy soil quickly, and he pulls out something covered in plastic, about the size of a telephone book. After he takes off a couple of layers of plastic, he's down to a box. I try not to show anything on my face, but I hope the women will be nice to look at, like the ones in the paintings.

'Hold the flashlight over here,' he says. The flashlight is like a spotlight. He takes the top off the box, and I shine the light in.

It's not women at all. It's a photograph of a man lying on his back, on top of some green plants. His eyes and mouth are open, but part of the top of his head is gone.

He's dead. I know he's dead. Howard pulls out another picture. It's a hand, not attached to anything. And then another, with four bodies, covered in blood.

'They're horrible,' I say. I feel sick, and I can feel my heart beating. I don't want to see the pictures, and I don't want to see Howard's face.

'They're amazing,' he says. He's breathing hard through his mouth, licking his lips. He looks ugly.

'Hey! Give me the flashlight if you're not going to shine it right.'

'Howard, those are real people.'

'They are not. They're the enemy. They're Viet Cong.'

'I'm going back to the boat. Hurry up, Howard, or I'll be grounded forever.'

The lights are coming on in some of the houses. I push the boat out so that the sharp end is barely resting on the shore, and hold it as it bobs about. Still, there's no sign of Howard. I could get in and row back and leave him there. I could tell my mom or his mom about the pictures, and how he makes me do things I don't want to do, and how he bullies his brothers and sisters. I wonder if my mom would be angry at me, or concerned about me instead of just thinking of herself for a change. I know that I'm not brave enough to leave without Howard. I can hear his heavy footsteps coming, and when I turn around he shines the flashlight in my face.

'Okay, Spanky. Get in and start rowing. You're not going to tell anyone, are you?'

'No. Course not.'

I row as hard as I can toward the lights at Howard's house. I still feel sick and clammy. I'm glad it's too dark to see Howard now. When we get back to his house, I jump out of the boat as soon as we hit shore. We don't say a word to each other, and I run along the shoreline to my house, trying to figure out what I'll say to my mom. I open the door with my key. There are no lights on, but the phone is ringing. I don't even stop at the door to pull my sandy shoes off. I feel my way through the half-dark to get to the phone before it stops ringing. It's my mom.

'I'm sorry, honey,' she says. 'I'm just leaving work. I'll be home in about fifteen minutes.'

I hang up my coat, and start peeling the potatoes. I'll have time to have a cup of tea ready for her when she comes in the door.

Sally Ann Wishes
Autumn 1965

Dear Diary,

I wish I lived in town, and not on this sad bleak lake. The sky is grey and it feels like it's squashing down on me. The water is grey, too, at the edges and where skims of ice are forming—spreading. They'll all join up by the end of the month and the lake will be sealed over until spring. Then, when it snows, it will look blank, and when the sun manages to come out the glare of the ice and the glittering of the snow will hurt too much to let you look at it, so it might as well not bother. I hate this place in winter.

I wish I didn't have to be on this school bus. It's 8:21 and I'm sitting here waiting for something to happen so I can write it in you, dear diary. ANYTHING. It's chaos in the afternoon on the way home, but mornings, nobody wants to be awake. Nobody wants to be here.

The cool kids sit at the back. It's like there's a magic door dividing the bus, and you have to be brave to attempt to pass through. Sometimes kids try and when the barrier comes up to stop them they die a little—right in front of everybody. Most of us aren't that stupid.

I'm sitting toward the front, over a wheel. It feels a little bit buzzy here, so it's not a popular spot. It doesn't help my handwriting, but it means everyone leaves me alone.

I'm by the window, and next to me is Frieda. She's a couple years older than me, so she has to ignore me. She has a little pink compact, and keeps powdering her nose, but really she's looking in the mirror to see what's going on at the back of the bus. She thinks they don't know, but I'm sure they'll work it out, and then they will laugh at her again.

One day last month she tried to sit at the back, a couple of rows up. They started: 'Hey, Frieda.' 'How's it going, Frieda?' Every time they said her name they made it sound like a dirty word. When the bus pulled up to the junior high school where all the older kids got out, everybody was watching to see what would happen. Usually everyone waits for the cool kids to get out. It's like a little show for us all when they pour out, looking like they don't care about anything. But that day they just waited. Mr. Fletcher the bus driver was getting annoyed, drumming his fingers on his big steering wheel and sighing out loud. Finally he said, 'Come on, kids. We haven't got all day,' and Betsy, at the back, said, 'Yeah, Frieda, come on,' and Francine said, 'Make a move, girl.' Finally Frieda got up and walked up the aisle by herself. Then all the back seat kids clapped. So did some of the other kids who probably wished they were popular, too. Frieda's face was red and she looked like she was trying not to cry. I bet that would have made them happy.

Why would anybody want to be popular? Especially if you have to be cold and heartless. I wouldn't wish that on anybody.

Sally Ann xx

Fire and Blood
Late Autumn 1965

We lived in the kind of home where everyone usually tried to be somewhere else. My older brothers were out on the lake all summer. They stayed at school playing football and basketball, or at friend's houses. When they were home they were closed up in their bedroom. They had each other, which must have been nice. If they ever argued, I didn't know about it. My mother worked part-time until my Dad lost his job, when I was about seven. Then she started full-time in a factory. She said it was boring and degrading. Whenever she was home she was boiling with rage, and she hissed at us every chance she got.

After a while she decided to give up that job. She worked as a checkout lady at a supermarket, and because the pay was bad she also worked in a bar in town three or four nights a week. Dad couldn't understand how the checkout job was better than the factory, and he hated her working in the bar, but she said the new arrangement suited her fine.

Dad spent most of his time hiding in his workshop behind the garage. I never thought to wonder what he was doing out there. The day I saw him with the cigarette, I had been at a friend's house. When I came home I rang the doorbell to be let in, but no one came. After a few minutes I walked around to the back door. There was no answer to my knocking, so I went to the little window of Dad's workshop. I remember it as though I'm looking at a series of photographs, and can stop and see each moment in detail.

He was sitting on one of those metal folding chairs. He had taken his shirt off, which seemed odd. He was holding something little in the fingers of his right hand, and was staring at it. He put his left arm in front of him, bent at the elbow. Then he slowly brought the thing in his right hand closer and closer to the inside of his left arm, his eyes going from the thing in his fingers to his arm, back and forth, over and over. He was taking deep breaths, so deep that his head rocked back a bit each time. I can't remember at what point I realized that the little thing in his right hand was a lit cigarette. I think there was a moment when I tried to convince myself that my eyes weren't seeing what they were seeing. When the cigarette touched his skin it was as if the pain was going through me—not real pain, but a shock, like electricity. He looked up and saw me, and his eyes were panicky. There was the window between us, but he seemed to be saying 'Oh, no, Charlie, no Charlie.' I can't be sure now if that's what he was saying or if I imagined that part. I can remember feeling afraid of him then, although I knew he would never hurt me. Maybe I was afraid *for* him. I ran to the far end of the yard, behind some bushes. I was too old to hide like that, I know. I could see him through the thick leaves, buttoning his shirt as he searched for me.

'Come on, Charlie. Come out so I can talk to you.'

I couldn't imagine how Dad would make sense of this, but I knew I couldn't stay behind the bush forever, so I came out of my hiding place. He had a pleading sound in his voice. Maybe some of what I remember as his words was me filling in the blanks later. But I'm sure I remember him saying that it was something that he had to do, and that I must not tell my mother—she would never understand. I never saw him burn himself again.

My mother's anger carried on at its usual pitch. I think the fact that Dad never fought back made her more angry. A few months after the burning, things finished falling apart between my parents and Dad moved out. I've never seen him since. I tell myself that he's alive, and living a safe, quiet life somewhere. I used to hope that he'd come back for me when I was eighteen, and my mother couldn't stop me going with him. That's three years from now, but I don't think it will happen.

For a while my mother went on and on about what a bad husband/bad father/bad person he was. When her anger finally wound down she didn't bother talking about him any more. By then a lot of my memories of him had become confused, what with me trying to make sense of everything, mingled with my mother's poisonous rants. Things didn't get worse. They just got more and more empty.

When I was about thirteen my mother started becoming a lot more pointed about my own shortcomings. What it boiled down to was that she didn't like the kind of person I was growing into. Maybe I reminded her of Dad, or maybe in her own way she wanted to make me a better person. I envied the kids at school who were happy and seemed to get along with others easily. I'd have changed to make myself more like them if I knew how.

The first time for me was a Saturday evening last year. My brothers had both moved out by that time, and my mother was at work. At eight o'clock the dance had started at school, and I was at home, flipping around the TV channels. I was feeling sorry for myself. Pathetic, I know. I noticed the ashtray on the coffee table, full of my mother's cigarette ends. I fished out the longest one, and got a book of matches from the kitchen. I spent a while thinking about things, and then went into the kitchen, got the scissors and snipped my mother's lipstick print from the filter. That seemed to make me stronger, more resolute. I slipped off my shirt, and looked at the sickly color of my inner arm. It seemed such a private place. I wondered what the imprint of a cigarette would look like, a wet red sore that I could watch change to a scar—whiter and purer than my own color.

I'd like to say that I was brave and deliberate that first time, but I wasn't. I barely touched my skin, and shrieked with the pain. Then I was aware of the stink of my mother's cigarette on my hand. I stood in the shower, washing and crying, and sheltering my silly little burn from the spray of water. I decided I'd have to work to become stronger.

I spent the whole week thinking and planning. It was exciting, having the secret, and building up my willpower. It was the most in-control I'd ever felt. The next Saturday evening I waited until dusk, and went out to my Dad's old workshop. I lit a couple of candles, and watched them burn. When I closed my eyes I could still see the flames, as if they were imprinted on the inside of my eyelids, giving me strength. I passed my hand over the flame again and again, never really burning myself, just building my courage. I thought about my dad, and how I wished he were still a part of my life. His toolbox was on the floor. I brushed away the dust and cobwebs, and lifted the top open, searching through the jumble until I found his utility knife. I passed the blade slowly through the flame of one of the candles, and pushed up my left sleeve. The blade slid easily through my skin near the little burn. I let the drops of blood run onto the back of my right hand. I held it up to watch the red drips trace along the vein lines, within me and without. It felt good, being so much in touch with myself.

Now, I'm not aware of pain when I'm cutting. My mind is too busy concentrating on my need to feel it. And afterwards, the pain reminds me of the secret, and the relief. My blood is sweet and sticky. It's such a bright red, seeing it gives me power. I got into the habit of cutting whenever I needed to get in control, and no one has ever found out.

A few weeks ago I took a book out of the library. It was a photographic record of the twentieth century. Toward the back of the book there was a black-and-white picture of a Buddhist monk. He was sitting on the ground—you could see him clearly through the huge ball of flames. He was making a sacrifice of himself in protest. I cleaned the blade of Dad's utility knife, and carefully cut the picture out of the book so no one would miss it. I keep it in Dad's workshop. It's hypnotic, looking at each of the hundreds of little feathers of flame, and focusing on his face. I would never have imagined anyone could be so courageous. He must have made the authorities ashamed.

We have a full can of gasoline for the lawn mower in the garage. I love its cold metallic smell. I sit and think of the magic it can create with the touch of a lighted match. And I feel braver, more sure of myself with each passing day.

A Million Miles from Cecile
Winter 1965

The whole Françoise Sagan thing started last winter, when I was fifteen—young and stupid. You think life can't get any more humiliating, but there's always something around the corner.

Her book was called *Bonjour Tristesse*. Monnie bought it for a book report. She wouldn't normally waste money buying a book, but she had a voucher to use up from her birthday. She said she liked the French-ness of the title. Her name is really 'Monique,' after her old French grand-maman, so she has a thing about France. And the book was short, a big plus.

She didn't much like it. It had the word 'melancholy' in the first line, so she knew it wasn't for her. I don't think she read more than the paragraph on the back and the first line. The spine wasn't even cracked. She got a D on the book report, which was probably generous of Mrs. Mackie. Then Monnie gave the book to me.

'Why would I want to read stuff like that? For crying out loud!' she said. Monnie is always dramatic. She'd make a terrific Miss America, with her 'isn't life wonderful' attitude and her big roomy smile. We're like the attraction of opposites in friends. She tries to cheer me up, and feels good because she's done this virtuous thing, and she thinks I'm deep, because I listen to her, and I like sad stories that make me cry. Living in Brighton is boring. Nothing ever happens. All those lakes all over and we're stuck in town. So if a novel can take me somewhere else I'm happy to jump in.

The book was perfect for me. 'Bonjour Tristesse' actually means hello sadness, and Françoise Sagan was only eighteen when she wrote it. Imagine that.

I got sucked into the book. Cecile, the girl who's telling the story, is so sure of herself. She controls the adults around her by outsmarting and out-manipulating them. I loved that. I'm afraid of everything. My mom says I need to grow up. She just makes things worse. I think I'm an embarrassment to her. 'Stand up straight. Don't slouch,' she says. I'm plain and skinny. And flat chested, not all curves like Mom. And I spend a lot of the time being miserable, probably because I'm plain and skinny. She'd have liked a daughter like Monnie. Who wouldn't?

I read the book in November. We had a couple of inches of dirty snow on the ground, so it was like a vacation, reading about hot French sunshine. Before it got to the really sad stuff, while Cecile was being care-free and sophisticated, there's this part where she comes downstairs in her pajamas and has an orange and a cup of black coffee for her breakfast. I thought that was so cool. I tried it. I needed three sugars. I wanted to *be* Cecile, with her way of explaining her feelings, her older man boyfriend, Malcolm, and her handsome, romantic father who adored her. And I was just boring Maurine from Small Town, USA with no social life and a bald electrician for a dad. Cecile drank whiskey and smoked and drove to a casino in Cannes. I drank coke or Kool Aid, and had to have my mom drive me everywhere. Cecile's mom died when she was little, and she didn't even miss her.

I decided I needed to have what Mrs. Mackie called an interior life. I would never be a butterfly like Monnie, but I thought if I tried I might develop into a passable moth. Moths can fly.

They used to have these diaries you could buy that had a tiny lock and key, so you could write whatever you liked and it would be private, but when I looked for them I couldn't find any. I bought a dark green spiral notebook at the dime store. I figured Cecile wouldn't like a fancy diary anyway. I kept it at the bottom of my sweater drawer. I didn't write in it for a week. I couldn't think of anything to say.

The day I finally started to write in it started out weird. I woke up in the night. I could hear my mom and dad's voices, but it was pitch black. It was like I didn't even have my eyes open. And it was cold. Biting. What had woke me up was my dad tripping over something in the living room and shouting 'merde.' Actually, he said the English word for it. I called out, 'What's going on?' and Mom said, 'The electricity's out. Stay in bed and keep warm.'

I thought great. Maybe there would be no school. After a few minutes, Dad came bumbling back with a flashlight. The cold was already seeping through my blanket, so I got up and felt around for my robe. I looked out my window, but it was black. I put on some socks and went back to bed. Then I started thinking about my diary. I thought maybe I should start with one of those unrhyming poems, about starting the fresh clean pages and promising to write in it every day no matter what.

When I woke up it was light out. My clock radio was still stopped at 2 a.m.. My watch said eight-fifteen. I would normally have already left for school. I got up and went to the window. Everything was shiny white, with a thick coating of ice on top of the snow. Big branches of trees were broken, and bushes were bent to the ground. I quickly put my clothes on over my pajamas, pulled on an extra sweater and my ski socks. I put my robe on over my clothes, and got back in bed with a bright green ink pen and my diary.

The world is clean and brand new.
I'm ready to start the rest of my life.

Then I went downstairs to find something for breakfast.

It was three days before they opened school again, and I didn't get as far as the front door. I slipped on a patch of ice that was lurking somewhere between the scattered rock salt, and landed on the side of my head. I sliced the top of my ear on the sidewalk. What with the shock of the pain, and having the wind knocked out of me, I just lay there. Of all people, the beautiful Mark Caruso scooped me up, collected my books and stuff, and whisked me to the school office. I was then taken to the hospital to get my ear stitched back together. My mom met me at the hospital. She'd been told it was nothing serious, but she needed to be there before they would sew me up. I knew she wouldn't be happy about being called away from work, but she seemed genuinely impressed by the amount of blood all over my scarf and jacket. I left the hospital with five stitches, a big bandage over my ear, and instructions not to wash my hair until the stitches had been removed.

I talked my mom into letting me stay home from school the next day to get over the shock and blood loss. Then I wore a big woolly hat. It was hot and made my head itch, but I couldn't bear to be seen with slimy hair and a stitchy ear. Back in school, I ran into Mark Caruso three times the first day. I normally saw him that often, but he'd never noticed me before. Now it was all, 'How's it going?', 'You sure bleed a lot.', 'Nice hat.' The third time he passed me in the hall he winked at me. I knew I wasn't in his league and he was just carrying through on the hero thing, but it felt good—better than you can imagine.

While all this was going on, I occasionally thought, at least I'll have something to write in my diary. I couldn't imagine any of it happening to Cecile, but I thought maybe she grew up a lot between my age and when the book happened.

When I got home I grabbed an apple and a Snickers bar and headed for my bedroom. I wanted to get some writing done before my mom got home from work.

I lit my jasmine candle. My desk was covered with stuff, so I took my diary from my drawer and propped myself up on my bed. Oh, that bed. What had I been thinking two years ago when I'd asked for a bed with a canopy? The bed was okay, but the giant lace doily on top looked like something out of *Gone With the Wind.*

'I knew you'd love it,' my mom had said. She *so* has no idea. I wondered what motherless Cecile's room was like.

I started writing. I wrote about the first time I'd seen Mark Caruso that day, and the second time. When I got to the last time, and the wink, I didn't leave it there. I wrote that he had stopped to talk to me, had offered to carry my books home after school. I started writing lots of things. It was magic. I could almost imagine I was writing about real stuff. I forgot the time. I didn't even hear my mom get home until she burst into my room without knocking.

'What are you doing with your door closed?'

'I'm doing homework,' I said. 'We're writing fiction in English.' I had this horrible feeling she might ask to read it, but she just looked at me like she does when she's trying to see if I look guilty about something, and then told me to set the table when I finished that part of my homework.

The next day at school when I passed Mark Caruso in the hall, he nodded at me the first time. After that, I went back to being invisible. It was comforting to know I'd be able to return to the relationship we had in my notebook.

There was something exciting about putting all those fantasies down on paper. It made them feel real. I got carried away. I started writing total fiction, with me as the not so ordinary main character and Mark Caruso as the smitten one.

By the time my stitches were out and I was able to shed my hat, notebook-Mark and I had gone too far. I wrote about how he was so sorry, but just couldn't stop himself. I wrote that he swore he would stand by me, no matter what, and that he had promised to quit school and get a job if I turned out to be pregnant, that we couldn't kill a baby that was part of both of us. He paced the room as he talked, and I lay tragically on my bed. After a few days of that, I couldn't think of anything else to write. The whole thing started to make me feel hollow. I tried reading *Bonjour Tristesse* again, but the shine had gone off that, too.

I hadn't seen much of Monnie since I fell and cut my ear. I'd wondered if she'd finally decided I just wasn't cool enough, what with the woolly hat and everything. A few days after I stopped writing in the notebook, she came to my locker as I was putting my coat on to go home.

'You want to walk home together?' she asked.

It had rained most of the day, and we walked out into a blowy afternoon, more like March than December. It's fantastic when all the snow is gone, and it's warm enough to start smelling things again; things like those big purple flowers, and even the waterlogged worms on the sidewalk.

Monnie told me about some new boy she'd met at her church. She liked to tell me about her love life. When I thought about it, most of our conversations were her telling me about boys and what they did or how nice they were to her. For the first time I wondered if there might have been a touch of fiction to what she told me. Then I felt bad, like I'd had an evil thought about her, and all she was doing was being nice to someone she didn't even have to bother with.

I could see my mom's car in the drive when I turned the corner. I had forgotten it was Wednesday, her day off. I liked it better when I had the house to myself. When I walked in the front door, she was sitting in the middle of the couch with my green spiral notebook in her hand.

'What is this?' she said. She was so angry her voice was shaking. It felt like my heart was beating in my ears.

'You went in my drawer.'

'Never mind that. Why didn't you come to talk to me about this? I didn't even know you were...active.'

There were too many things whizzing around in my head to get them straight—the snooping, the embarrassment and shame, the fact that I'd have to admit that I made the whole thing up. She started again.

'I think we'd better go and meet this Mark Caruso and his parents. How far along are you? God, how will I tell your father? To think what went on in my house when I was out at work.'

'Mom, it's made up. It's just writing.'

'Don't lie to me.'

'I'm not.' I was crying by this time. 'I hardly know him.'

'Well,' she said in her dubious voice, 'we'll know soon enough if you're lying, won't we?' I wasn't sure which lying she meant.

'Don't tell Dad. Please. It's too humiliating.' I went to my bedroom before she said anything else. I lay on my bed with Sagan's book. I wanted to tear the stupid thing up, but I didn't have the energy.

I don't know what mom did with my notebook. I know she told my dad because of the way he looked at me for a while, like he didn't know who I was any more. I would think about them talking to each other about me. They have each other. Monnie has anyone she wants. Even Cecile had her Malcolm.

I bought this notebook at the same store I bought the green one. I thought the navy blue looked somber. If you're reading this, Mom, I hope you understand how much I hurt, that I'm just as sad as poor motherless Cecile.

Ice
Late Winter 1965

What you're supposed to do is throw your arms straight out at your sides. That's what stops you falling all the way through the ice. All the grown-ups used to say that before they let any of us kids out to skate on the lake at Grandpa and Grandma's house. And they'd say it with their eyebrows raised, almost shaking a finger, in the same voice they used for saying, 'Don't talk to strangers.'

Grandpa used to check with the men who fished. They'd chip holes in the ice about as big around as a basketball, and then pitch their little shanties to shelter from the wind. Then they'd drop their lines deep into the water to catch the big fish that lurked at the bottom. And they'd always take tape measures so they could see how thick the ice was. They'd report back, ten inches, or thirteen inches, or whatever. Dad told me about one really cold winter before I was born when the ice got to twenty-one inches. Anyway, they wouldn't allow us kids out on the ice until late December, when it was eight inches or more. And we'd have to stay on a patch close to shore where Dad and Grandpa would have cleared the snow away.

Mom would wrap us up in sweaters and coats, scarves and mittens, and a couple of pairs of socks, so that by the time we got outside I'd feel like I was swimming in syrup. It was only when I'd get out on the ice and start to skate that the muffled up feeling would go, and I'd race as fast as I could, back and forth, again and again. I'd have to be careful if my little sister Maddie was out. Grandpa always said that girls were fragile, and we had to treat them like glass. That didn't sound like Maddie. She was always slow and clumsy, and would get mad if I whizzed by too close.

Then last winter, when I was ten, Dad started treating me differently, like I was more grown up. He took me with him to the lake to visit Grandpa and Grandma a couple of times, and Mom and Maddie stayed home. We talked about a lot of things on the way—things like football and cars. In November he showed me how to use some of the tools in his workshop. We made a wooden nesting box together, and I gave it to Grandpa for Christmas.

And after the Christmas turkey, when Mom and Grandma were clearing the table, Dad and Grandpa and I set off to walk all the way around the lake. It took over two hours, and it was starting to get dark by the time we got back. I tried not to jabber on like a little kid, and I listened to them talking. I remember, we were on the other side of the lake near the campgrounds, and it was deserted. There was just hard old snow and bare trees where in the summer it was always busy as an anthill. I was thinking that Dad and Grandpa were probably thinking the same thing as me when Grandpa started to laugh. He inched his way a few feet out over the ice and turned to Dad.

'You know,' he said, 'I haven't thought of this for years. The first summer we came camping here you were no more than a baby. We used to bring an old enamel washtub and fill it with lake water. We'd sit you in the tub and you would splash and splash until it was empty. Then we'd fill it up again and you'd do the same thing, over and over. You'd spend the whole morning, just splashing in your own private lake. I never dreamed then that we'd be lucky enough to live here when I retired. Most of the houses around the lake hadn't even been built then. It was more like a wilderness, untouched. The trees grew right to the shoreline. Imagine. And the fishing was out of this world. Remember me teaching you to fish, son? You, on the shore with a bamboo pole, waiting for your dad to bait your hook for you?'

Grandpa stood, laughing and shaking his head, the same way Dad always did when he found something surprising. Then Dad turned his sheepish smile at me, as if he was embarrassed to think of me imagining that baby in the washtub, or the little boy needing his dad's help to put a worm on a hook. I didn't think my dad had ever been afraid of anything.

'Come on, Dad,' he said. 'My feet are starting to feel numb.'

As we crunched over the frozen snow, I tried to see that baby and the washtub in my mind. I tried to imagine Grandpa as a dad, younger than my dad. I guess up to that point I had thought of them as having always been grown-ups who understood just how the world worked.

It happened a few months later. It was the middle of March, that horrible in-between time that's so boring. The ice was starting to melt so we couldn't skate or ice-fish and summer swimming was still a million years away.

I was skimming stones along the ice, trying to get it just right so they carried on for a long way, but they kept stopping when they'd hit a wet patch. Dad and Grandpa were sitting on the little wall that divides the front yard from the sand and the lake. They were talking about the dock they planned to build, trying to decide what length would be best.

'We'll have to make sure Maddie knows she can't go out on it without an adult,' Grandpa said.

'I have this vision of you,' Dad said, 'sitting at the end of the dock in your rocking chair, fishing from morning to night.'

'Sounds good to me, son.'

I was thinking, Grandpa and Dad would enjoy making the dock together as much as sitting on it once it was finished. I was wondering if they would let me help, maybe paint it before they put it out on the lake. Even though it was cold, I could feel the warmth of the sun on my shoulders. I'd found a stick, and was burrowing under the edge of the lake, chipping away where the ice was starting to melt. We heard a high whining sound from the far side of the lake. I loved the way sounds travelled over the ice, like they were rushing to meet you.

'Is that a saw?' Dad asked. 'Funny time of year to be trimming trees.'

Then we saw it, coming fast across the ice.

'Skidoodle!' I said, once I realized what it was. That's what Maddie always called the snowmobiles, and everyone always laughed when she said it. But they didn't seem to hear me.

'What an idiot!' Grandpa said. 'Surely he must know the ice is too thin, and too wet! He must be crazy!'

The driver of the snowmobile kept zigzagging around, splashing through big watery patches, and skidding as he turned and then picked up speed again.

'He's going so fast, he might just get away with it,' Dad said. Then the snowmobile came closer to our side of the lake. Dad and Grandpa started waving their arms and shouting for him to come in shore to safety. His engine was so loud, I'm sure he didn't hear them, but he must have realized by the way they were waving their arms that something was wrong.

Dad shouted, 'Look! He's no more than a kid. What are his parents doing, letting him out on that thing in these conditions?'

The machine turned away from us, and skimmed off again. As the sharp sound of its motor faded we could hear the strange pinging noises the ice sometimes makes, echoing around. The snowmobile disappeared behind the little island on the far side of the lake.

Dad had just got back to talking about the dock, when the whining started again. We looked over to watch it coming straight across the lake toward us, fast. Then it was like watching in slow motion. It hit a wet patch, spraying water, and left the surface of the lake—flew up in the air and crashed down sideways, throwing its driver onto the ice.

Grandpa said, 'Good God, God almighty,' again and again under his breath. We waited for the driver to get up, but he didn't.

Some of Grandpa's neighbors came out of their houses and joined us on the shore. They must have been watching the whole thing from inside. A bald man said he had called the police. The ice was making lots of eerie pinging, twanging noises, and we could hear muffled cracking sounds running through it. Time seemed to stop moving. The grown ups kept saying the same things, like how awful it was, and how the person on the ice wasn't moving.

'We can't just stand here and wait for them to arrive,' my dad said.

'Hey,' the bald man said. 'I've got a rope. Someone can hold onto the end of it and edge his way out.'

'Don't be an idiot. It would have to be seventy, eighty yards. You don't have a rope that long,' Grandpa said. I'd never heard him talk to anyone like that. Everything seemed unreal, the man on the ice, the grown-ups arguing, and the crashed snowmobile's engine still screaming away. I could hardly see the person on the ice. Dad kept shaking his head, like he couldn't believe what was happening. Then he started saying, 'Stupid kid. Stupid kid.' Grandpa turned back and looked toward the road up the hill when we heard a car, but it didn't stop. He said, 'Surely we should be hearing a siren by now.'

Then Dad started walking out over the ice, slowly and crouched right over. Grandpa was shouting at him to come back, but he didn't stop. Grandpa started praying, saying, 'please God' and 'oh, dear God.' I should have shouted. In my mind I was screaming, 'Come back, Dad. Let someone else help.' But my voice came out thin and weak. I wanted to reach out over the ice and pull him back. It was a silly thing to think, that you could make a connection like that.

He didn't turn around. He started to look so small, on the wide grey of the lake.

Then, when he was more than half way out, he went down and disappeared under the ice. I don't know if he put his arms out to try to stop himself. I try not to think about any of the things that happened that day. I'd spent my whole lifetime with Dad, but every time I think about him, I come back to that day.

Grandpa and Grandma are staying with us now. They're selling their house on the lake. Grandma says she can't bear looking out at it. Everyone is sad, and some people have told me my dad was a hero, but it doesn't seem like that to me. The police helicopter came and rescued the kid—even saved his stupid snowmobile. But it took them a long time to find my dad.

Amanda
Early Spring 1966

Amanda opened her curtains to let in the weak March light. She wished she could see the lake from her bedroom, but she was tucked away at the back of the house. Still, she could see the buds on the beech tree, the promise of change.

Then she heard her mother's bell from down the hall. That 'cheated' feeling flooded back. The bell was shrill and insistent. She walked down the hall to her mother's room.

'Why did you make me wait?' the woman rasped. 'If I exhaust myself first thing in the morning, I'll be spent before lunch.'

Amanda set her mother's slippers beside the bed and brought the red Japanese kimono from the hook on the door. The seam was giving way at one of its arms. She wouldn't mend it until her mother noticed. She remembered when her father had brought it back from Tokyo, where he had attended a dental conference almost twenty years ago. A green dragon danced across the back. Amanda had wondered as a girl if her dad's choice of gift for his wife had been a bold stab at humor.

'Open the blinds, will you? I want to see the lake. Help me with my legs. I need the lav. Quickly.'

Amanda never would have imagined she'd see the day when her mother would be anything but strong. She had been a big woman who strode rather than walked through life. Then, in her late sixties, she'd been swiftly diminished by a stomach complaint that turned out to be 'the big C.' (The word was never mentioned, as if to not acknowledge it would minimize its harm.) Operations were performed, bits were removed, and still, the big C battled on. Now, the doctor had said it was a matter of time. Amanda would have liked to know how much time. She didn't exactly wish her mother gone, but it would help if she knew how long they were to be suspended together in this nether-life. Big C or no big C, her mother wouldn't go without a fight.

Amanda hated mornings most. It took almost two hours to get her mother up and showered, sitting on a plastic chair in the cubicle. Amanda would end up drenched. She peeled her clothes off and wore her terry bathrobe until her chance for a quick shower after breakfast.

This morning, by the time she returned to her room she was in a miserable mood. There was no point in complaining. Theirs was a one-way relationship when it came to the venting of feelings. Her mother had moved from her usual tetchiness to odd vagueness over breakfast. She seemed to have forgotten why she was sitting at the table. Now she was having a rest back in bed. Amanda allowed herself extra time in the shower, letting the hot water run down her neck and back. She tried to think herself into some other place, but she'd found the sicker her mother became, the harder it was to access her imagination. So she stood, breathing in the steam for a moment longer, before stepping out of the shower.

She thought she heard her mother's wretched hand bell again and stopped a minute to listen, but no. The house was quiet. It was past noon, and she remembered that the nurse had said she would stop by in the afternoon for a blood sample. There were days when Amanda spoke to no one but her mother. She hummed as she dressed, then went to her mother's room.

From the hallway she could see the bell on the floor, along with a broken glass sitting over a puddle of water. Her mother's arm was stretched across the table, her face wedged down between the bed and the nightstand. Amanda knew that she was dead, but couldn't touch her, or turn her over. She stood in the doorway, trying to figure out what was expected of her. She felt elated, and then shame washed over her. She edged a few steps closer, and was relieved by the sound of the doorbell. She rushed downstairs and opened the door to the nurse.

'I've just gone in to her.' Her voice sounded breathless. 'I think she's...gone.' She couldn't bring herself to use the real word, though it seemed to hang in the air before her.

The nurse, a short, masculine woman, stepped past Amanda and climbed the stairs.

'Just wait there for the moment, dear,' she said over her shoulder.

It took a while before Amanda realized she was still standing holding the front door open. She closed it. What had she been doing when her mother had tried to call her? Was she standing in the shower, imagining herself anywhere else? What must the nurse think, finding her mother like that? And what did Amanda need to do next? Ring people? Her sister first? She wanted someone to take charge.

'Come upstairs, dear.' The nurse was standing at the top of the stairs. Amanda climbed obediently upwards.

The nurse had put her mother straight in the bed, one of her hands resting on the other over the tidied covers; the broken glass had been cleared away. Amanda felt glued to her spot by the door. The nurse took her by the hand, guided her to the bedside. The woman reached over and smoothed some wires of grey hair from her mother's forehead.

'She's at peace now,' the nurse said. 'You can kiss her.'

She heard herself gasp 'Certainly not!' She was taken aback by the ugliness of the idea, but she hadn't meant to say it out loud. The nurse looked startled. The room was stifling. Amanda wasn't sure if it was her mother's spirit that filled the room, sucking away the oxygen. She turned to the window, opened it wide, letting in cold, clean air.

*

Amanda somehow managed to organize the funeral and invite the guests. Would you call them guests? Would you have called the hours afterward at the house a wake? The day of the funeral was long, the church service at 10.00, then the drive to the cemetery in Detroit where her mother was laid to rest next to her dad - ashes to ashes, dust to dust. That was when Amanda had registered the reality of it all. Her mother was gone, surely and finally. It was such a stunning thought. She'd felt all the eyes on her, and in the church, too. Her mind was jumping back to memories and forward to some unknown future. She tried to concentrate.

There was a rustle and shift among the congregation as her mother's friend Megan returned to her seat. Amanda had missed the entire eulogy.

Everyone had loved her mother; brave bold Vera. Even her name sounded fierce. But she was fierce in a positive way, Amanda thought. She closed her eyes. Sometimes she wasn't sure if her thoughts were her own, or what she had been taught to think. Now she would be able to stop the constant battle of squelching down what she actually felt.

After the service Vera's small house was stuffed with people.

'She wouldn't have wanted to linger.'

'The stroke was a blessing. At least she isn't suffering.'

Megan helped her carry used glasses and plates to the kitchen. Both of her brothers and her sister were holding forth, dotted among the guests. They must have figured that dishes washed themselves, teacups and wine glasses refilled automatically. As Megan rinsed and stacked, she said, 'Your mother touched so many lives.' Amanda thought it sounded like an echo of the earlier eulogy, but she couldn't be sure.

She opened her mouth to reply and the wrong words came out.

'Yes,' she said. 'She did cast a giant shadow.'

Megan looked shocked, but quickly recovered.

'A wonderful old tree,' Amanda tried. The words sounded odd to her as they left her mouth. She wondered if she'd had three glasses of sherry. She'd planned to limit herself to two, but even at this point wanted another desperately. And I'm not a drinker, she thought, and smiled at the possibility of taking it up.

'So, I suppose this house is yours now,' Megan said. 'You've been a good daughter, Amanda.'

People were putting away the garden chairs under the house. It had been too chilly to sit out, but most people had taken the opportunity to stand on the grass and look out at the lake. Almost all of the ice was gone. She'd heard a few people talking about the death three weeks before, the man who fell through the ice.

'So much tragedy,' her sister said. 'Two deaths on the same lake, so close together. That poor man, and now Mom. And they say tragedy comes in threes.' Amanda had thought how ridiculous, but had said nothing.

Later, when she opened the refrigerator she saw that someone had wrapped some of the leftover cheese and cold cuts. There were Tupperware containers she didn't recognise. They had notes on them. 'Tuna Bake. Eat by Friday.' 'Lasagna. You can freeze this one.' She didn't know the handwriting. There was a month's worth of cheese, and those little vegetable nibbles. She wondered if you could freeze cheese. She told herself she'd make some sort of soup tomorrow with the vegetables, and plenty of garlic. Her mother had always hated garlic.

She'd been sure she wouldn't sleep, but she had. She woke with the sound of the voices of children up at the school bus pick-up point. It was 8.15 by her alarm clock. She had usually been roused by her mother before 7.00. No more, she thought, turning the phrase over in her mind. She got up and dressed quickly, leaving her long hair loose on her

35

shoulders. She made herself a pot of tea, put on her coat and went out onto the porch. She perched on the top step for a long time, only getting up twice to go inside to refill her cup. What do people who don't live on water look at as they drink their morning tea? She couldn't imagine. She took her shoes and socks off, rolled her pants up to the knees and walked down to the lake. The shock of cold felt good. She slowly edged her way into the icy water, teacup in hand. It was too early in the year for the schools of minnows she supposed, but she stood still long enough for a little sunfish to swim up and stop inches from her. After a few minutes it swam up and gently nipped her numb leg before it glided off. Its brazenness made her laugh out loud. She poured the last drops of tea into the lake, and hurried back to the house.

Once her feet thawed, Amanda sat at the kitchen table and started to make a list. At the top she wrote, 'Get hair cut off.' Then she began a shopping list; she could buy whatever food she wanted.

Within a week Amanda went to work at the Little Skipper Inn, pouring coffee and serving short-order breakfasts to the morning customers. The house had long been paid for, and her needs were modest. She didn't plan to work there long, perhaps until the end of the summer season. She'd never considered what she would do with her life once her mother was gone, had felt that just letting herself think such things would be a kind of betrayal.

On Saturday, the young boy from three houses along came to her door. He said his mom had told him to come, to see if she needed any help with anything. She'd sent him away, then felt sorry that she had. It would have been nice to have someone to chat to. The next day, when he'd been walking along the edge of the lake past her house, she'd called him over.

'If you have the time I'd appreciate it if you'd rake my beach,' she said, and he seemed happy enough to do it. She'd given him a dollar. He'd looked down on it disappointedly, so she gave him two more.

'Let me know if I can do anything else,' he'd said.

She could always manage to find something to busy him. She liked the company. She boxed up some of her mother's things for the Salvation Army and he carried them to her car. He chatted a bit, shy at first, but he became more confident.

His name was Vincent. 'Like the painter,' she ventured, and he had smiled.

One of Those Kids from Up on the Hill
Late Spring 1966

You get sick of people thinking they know all about you before you get a chance to open your mouth. I'm one of those kids, labeled bad, and I've never known what I could do about it. The 'nice' people think they are so superior. They think they can say any rude thing when it comes to me and my family. They call my mom a bitch and a baby machine. They say we're a bunch of roughnecks. I've heard them.

Last September I was in the cafeteria eating my sandwich, and I accidentally knocked over my carton of milk. If anyone else did the same thing it wouldn't even be noticed. The teacher on lunch duty called me a punk. For knocking over my milk? He said it under his breath, but I heard it, and the other kids at the table heard it. Now kids call me Punky, and if I complain they say I'm being touchy.

Kids don't want to be my friend once they know who I am, and everyone knows who I am. They think I'm like my big brothers. It makes me mad. It's enough to make me want to do bad things, but that's not me. I want to make something of myself.

That's why I got interested in the trumpet. Mr. Dwyer from the junior high came to our school at the beginning of the year. He told us about their band program. They have a symphonic band, a jazz band, a marching band, and the seventh grade band. He said that even if we didn't play an instrument yet, if we worked hard we might get into the seventh grade band next year. He invited anyone who wanted to come to sit in on a marching band practice. I told Mr. Glenn, my teacher. He said it sounded like a way to get out of an hour or two of class, but he couldn't stop me going.

There were two girls and three boys from my school who decided to go. They picked us up in the junior high van, and took us over to the school. We went in a side door where there was a big lobby. On one side was the gym. I could hear kids playing basketball. Their shoes were making that squeaky noise, and there was shouting, 'Here, Bob, here,' and a teacher kept shouting, 'Who's guarding that player?' On the other side of the lobby was a room full of people singing together, and then there was the band room. You could hear them playing from the lobby, but when the door was opened for us to go in the music was ten times louder.

We stood by the door until they finished. Then they asked us to come in and join them. They sat me right in the middle of the trumpet section. I could feel the music in my chest. It seemed to zing around my rib cage and when it would well up, I swear I could hear it in my heart. It was the most exciting thing I felt in my whole life. I knew I wanted to play more than anything. Mr. Dwyer said, 'Of course, if you're starting out in the seventh grade band you won't sound this good,' and all the band members laughed. They looked like a fun bunch of kids.

I knew I was going to have trouble paying for lessons, so I wrote a letter to Mr. Dwyer and explained I was one of six kids without a dad. I was too young to even get a paper route to earn money to buy a trumpet and pay for lessons. He came back to my school and I was called to the principal's office. He was there waiting with Mr. Marcus, my school music teacher. They said they had been discussing me and had come up with a plan. I could borrow a trumpet from the junior high, just pay a $20 deposit, even though it costs a lot more than that. They said they had a fund for 'special cases'

'The school will pay for your lessons for the whole of sixth grade as long as you work hard at it,' Mr. Dwyer said. 'Then next year you will be able to get a paper route or something to pay for your lessons. And band practice will be forty minutes every day.' That was the first time I could remember someone doing something wonderful for me.

When I told my mom I wanted to take the trumpet she looked me in the eye and said the magic-killing word: money. I told her about the special fund and how much I wanted to do this. She said, 'We don't take charity, George.'

'It's not charity, Mom. I'll have to work really hard, and I really want to do it.'

'I don't remember ever seeing you get so excited about anything,' she said, and she smiled and said okay. She asked if I would be able to practice at school some of the time, because it was already noisy enough at home, but I think she was being funny. She ended up being pretty happy about the idea.

It was hard work until my mouth got used to it, and I got in control of the valves. I wanted to practice all the time. Mr. Marcus said I was a fast learner. He said he was impressed by my dedication. He said I needed to keep up with my regular schoolwork, too, though. At home I would make myself do any homework before I did trumpet. Then I'd go out to the garage and lock myself in and practice. When I'd finish I would feel calm and peaceful. The music would still play in my head, and I loved that.

The teachers at school started treating me better, like they weren't angry at me before I opened my mouth. I didn't care so much about the other kids either. Maybe it sounds crazy, but I felt like I had a purpose. I imagined myself in a couple of years time. I'd be in the marching band, and I would be surrounded by friends. It wouldn't matter that I'd have to go home to my sad shabby house where nothing gets fixed and there are always people who want to know my business. My two older brothers wouldn't be able to spoil everything. What I wanted most of all was to be in the jazz band. By the time I got to high school I would be good enough to be in any band. I would play

Sousa marches, and I would be part of symphonies. I knew I could do it, be part of something big and amazing. I knew this fire in me couldn't ever burn out.

I'm used to Howard. Mom says he teases everyone, but he's pretty harmless. He's not so bad in front of her, and I think she doesn't want to know the truth about him, that he is mean, and he enjoys being mean. It's what makes him happy. One of the things I liked about the trumpet was that it was mine and no one could take it away from me.

Sometimes one of us kids gets something from our dads, like a big box of candy, or a game or toy. Mom always says the best thing to do is share. Howard never gets a thing from his dad. Not even at Christmas. Mom used to give him a present on his birthdays and at Christmas and say it was from his dad. In the end he told her he knew it was from her. He could tell it was her handwriting on the cards. He told her to stop, that he'd rather just be mad at his dad than pretend he'd got stuff from him. I hate having to share, even though I try to be grown up about it. But the trumpet—how could I be expected to share that? When I first brought it home I let everyone have a turn at trying to make a musical sound, but they all just made noise and got tired of it. The little ones didn't have the power or the puff, (that's one of Mr. Dwyer's expressions). My older brothers made rude noised and laughed. Mom said they should stop. It wasn't a toy. She said that the trumpet wasn't even mine. It belonged to the school and was being loaned to me and I was responsible for it. She said no one but me was allowed to touch it after that.

Last Monday was my birthday, and my dad came to take me out to dinner. He drove us all the way into the city and we went to Big Boy's. I had a hamburger and a chocolate milkshake. When we were having desert I asked him if he would take me to his house so I'd know what it was like when I would think about him. It was hard to imagine. I didn't think I was asking for a lot. He said it wasn't possible, that he and his wife had a new baby son, and it wouldn't work out. He didn't look at me while he talked. He pushed his pie around on his plate. He looked sad, like he was the one being cheated. Even though I knew it was unfair, I didn't want him to be unhappy. If I said things that made him unhappy, maybe he wouldn't want to see me at all. I told him it didn't matter, and to change the subject I told him about the trumpet and Mr. Dwyer, and how he thought I was dedicated and doing really well. This evening was the first one in months that I didn't do my practice, and it would be too late when I'd get home because it might disturb the neighbors. But I said I'd do double practice the next day.

'Is that a fact?' he said. He said he used to play the clarinet, got all the way to level five. 'Maybe you get your musical talent from me, George,' he said, and he sounded proud.

He got me home by 9:00, like he'd promised. The little ones were in bed.

My big brothers were watching TV and Mom was doing the ironing.

'Did you have a good time?' Mom said.

I said yeah. I knew enough not to make a big deal of it in front of Howard, but he got up and left the room. I was waiting for a door to slam, but it didn't.

In the morning after my cereal, I went to the hall dresser to get my things for school. I had a history book and a spiral notebook, and of course, my trumpet in its case and my music book. The books were there, but the trumpet wasn't.

'Where is it?' I called out. 'Where's my trumpet?'

Mom was in bathroom helping my little brother brush his teeth.

'It's probably where you left it,' she shouted back.

'Probably where you left it,' Howard said in the whiny high-pitched voice he uses to mimic Mom. He was standing, leaning in the doorway. 'You should look after things better, Georgie boy. Where did you see it last? Did you leave it in the garage after you practiced last night? Oh, you didn't practice, did you?'

'I always leave it here except when I'm practicing. Always.' I was starting to get a sick feeling in my stomach. Howard stood there with that little smirk on his face.

'Well, last night was a special case. Maybe you did something different. Maybe you left it in the school bus. Who knows? Maybe you accidentally dropped it in the lake.'

When he said that I knew I'd never see it again. He said, 'You know, Mom won't believe you.' I ran outside, right down to the end of our dock. The water was murky. I couldn't see to the bottom.

On the bus on the way to school I realized Howard was too smart to have dropped it in the lake near the house. Maybe he had been planning for a long time. If I told on him, he would make my life hell, and Mom would stand by Howard. She always did.

I would have to tell Mr. Marcus. I would have to somehow pay for the trumpet, and they would never trust me with another one. Mr Dwyer would be angry or, worse still, disappointed. And I would never be able to feel what it's like to make music, to be part of that big magic thing.

I went straight to the office when we got to school. I told the secretary that I had lost my trumpet. She made that 'tsk' sound with her mouth, and told me she would tell Mr. Marcus when he came in. She told me to hurry to my class or I'd be late.

Later in the morning Mr. Marcus came to the classroom door. He talked to Mr. Glenn, and Mr. Glenn told me to go with Mr. Marcus for a chat. Mr. Marcus took me to the music room. There were music stands in a cluster in the corner but the room was empty.

'So,' he started, 'I understand you have lost the trumpet. How on earth did you manage to do that?' He didn't sound angry. He sounded tired. I felt ashamed, and angry that I had to feel ashamed for something I didn't even do.

'I don't know,' I said. 'I'm really really sorry.'

'You can't have lost it, George. We'll give it a day or two. I'm sure it will turn up.'

'No, it won't. I know it won't,' I said, and I began to cry. I couldn't stop myself.

Mr. Marcus has a way of waiting until you get something right, as if he knows you'll get there in the end. He let me cry, didn't try to comfort me, but didn't try to stop me either. I think someone started to come in the room, but he waved them away without saying a word. I got to the point that I didn't need to cry anymore, and we just sat a minute. Then Mr. Marcus said, 'I know!' like he'd had some brilliant idea. He went to a cupboard and got out a full sized saxophone and a trumpet. I don't know who they belonged to. He played a couple of scales on the sax. Then he started to play 'I Want to Hold Your Hand,' but he made it sound sad and soulful. He played 'Yesterday,' and the notes wandered around a bit like jazz.

He said, 'Feel free to join in.' I played a few notes when it felt right, not to sound smart, but just to be a part of it.

He didn't ask any more questions about the trumpet. He said, 'Look, George, I know that you have a lot to contend with. We'll sort something out.'

Now I have another trumpet, and I keep it at school. I practice an hour after school, and Mr Marcus drives me back and drops me at the top of the road. He says he's going to miss me when I move up from the junior high, but if I want, he'd be happy for me to drop in and play any time. I think in a year or so I'll give the saxophone a try. It sounds like it plays music straight from your soul.

Boys Don't
Late Spring 1966

Boys don't cry. Leon knows that. He's been told since he was small. His father doesn't allow tears. He says boys are hard and brave and do as they are told. Leon's dad used to be a sergeant in the army, and he would tell the recruits and the privates what to do and what to think. Then he stopped being a soldier and moved to Detroit where the jobs were, and he met Leon's mom, married her, and within a year Leon was born and ruined everything.

Leon knows what he should be like, what he should think and feel, but in his heart he knows he's not the person his dad wants him to be. Leon has a deep, deep well inside him. That's where he keeps his tears, and his anger and the hurt. He's not his father's little soldier.

Leon's dad can't seem to keep a job. This makes him angry. When he's angry he shouts. He shouts at his wife and his son, as if it were their fault. Sometimes he shouts at the neighbors. At their last house he shouted at the boys next door when they were noisy, or when their football came over the fence. He shouted when the neighbor's cat came into his yard. He threw a bottle at it and it smashed against the elm and it took a long time for Leon's mom to find all the pieces of glass. He threatened all sorts of terrible things that made the cat owner cry. The neighbors got together and had a meeting. They sent a letter to Leon's dad listing their complaints.

At about the same time Leon's dad had an argument with his foreman at the roller bearing factory. He had to go to his foreman's boss. Then he was told to leave the factory.

So now they are starting again, another job for Leon's father, another kitchen for Leon's mom, another school for Leon.

Leon is a shy, skinny boy with big elbows and knees. What he wants most is to be happy. He has been growing his hair longer, not exactly a Beatle cut, but long enough to be a bit wavy. What with the move and all, he missed his usual haircut, and his dad hasn't noticed. Leon wants the kids at the new school to think he's cool. It's hard jumping into the middle of 5th grade. He has to take the school bus, and everyone already has lots of friends, so he sits at the front of the bus and looks out the window. A lot of the kids live on lakes, and the school bus weaves from lake to lake after it picks him up.

The bus fills. Sometimes no one chooses to sit next to him. Other times one of the older kids does. Usually when that happens they spend the drive doing homework, frantic to get it done before they arrive. Sometimes Leon feels like he is invisible. Other times he wishes he was. His whole life has taken on a feeling of unreality. He can't wait to catch the bus in the mornings, and once he does, he can't wait to get off at the end of the school day. There is no one to talk to at school, and no one to talk to at home. And he can't get over what he heard late last night.

Hearing his dad shouting at his mom was not unusual, but last night she had shouted back, her voice high and hysterical. Then, right through the bedroom wall he heard the slap. Now Leon hears it over the rumble of the buses engine, over the sound of kids talking and laughing. He can feel his eyes filling with tears. He tries to blink them away, and feels one slide down his cheek. He turns to the window so no one can see, takes out a Kleenex to blow his nose and quickly wipes away the evidence.

More kids are piling onto the bus. He watches them sling book bags on their shoulders, juggle lunch boxes and sports bags. Not for the first time he chooses one person and tries to imagine what it would be like to be them. He usually chooses one of the boys, but they are a mystery to him. He can't imagine wanting to play baseball or basketball. He can't imagine having a tough attitude and being looked up to, like one or two boys in the fifth or sixth grade, or some of the junior high school boys, the ones whose names ring out as they get on the bus.

'Hey, Harry! Over here!'

'You ready for tomorrows game, Mike?'

'Tom, I've got some pictures of my dad's new boat. Come see.'

Today Leon chooses that girl from his class: Shannon, with the long dark hair and the nice sprinkle of freckles on her nose. What must it be like being Shannon? As she starts up the aisle it looks like she is going to sit next to him. He turns away, afraid she'll see his eyes are red. She sits across the aisle from him, next to an older girl. If he had been like any other boy she would have sat next to him. It's his own fault. He gets everything wrong. He can feel her watching him. He wishes he were invisible.

Something bad happens in class in the afternoon. It's Bobby Spicer's birthday. He has told everyone. Leon can see he thinks that makes him special. He says after school his family are going out for pizza, all three of his big brothers, his two best friends, and his parents of course. It's as if he can't sit still at his desk, he can't stop talking. Mrs Webster has told him to calm down again and again, but excitement seems to be bubbling up inside him, and he can't help himself.

Halfway through the afternoon Mrs Webster calls Bobby up to the front of the class. He gets up from his desk by the door, smiling, and walks up. Mrs Webster comes around her desk with a ruler in her hand. She tells him to put his hands out, palms up. She smacks each hand hard with the ruler. Bobby looks stunned, winces with each smack. She sends him back to his seat. Leon can hear him sniffing a few times. Leon feels his own eyes fill up again. Everyone else pretends like nothing has happened. Leon folds his arms on his desk and rests his forehead on his wrist.

'Leon,' Mrs Webster says, 'sit up properly in your seat.' Leon doesn't want to be seen.

'Leon, I said sit up.' She walks to his desk.

'What's wrong, Leon?'

He sits up. Everyone can see his blotchy red face, the streaky tears. He doesn't know if he's crying for Bobby or his mother or himself.

'Go to the lavatory and wash your face,' she says gently.

He obediently gets up and weaves his way through the desks to the door. As he passes Bobby he hears him whisper, 'Big baby.'

Strings
Late Spring 1966

Roy imagined them, had done since he was a boy. There were strings everywhere, linking each person to all the important people in their lives. He imagined tangles of strings reaching all over the world. Some people were weighed down by having so many. Some were sad because they had so few.

The string to his mother had been a fine gold chain. When she died it turned silver. Ghostly silver? Maybe that was it. His father was probably still alive, but they had long since lost touch. Still, there was a skinny frayed rope between them. Neither seemed to want to give it a tug.

Roy had never been big on friendship. There were some faint strings that trailed back to his boyhood, his twenties. Sometimes he wondered if the strings faded to nothing when you were forgotten. They had to go both ways. That made sense.

He knew his string to Betty would always be there. She had to see it sometimes when she looked at her son, because the child was his son, too. They'd been barely seventeen when he was born, and now the boy, Howard, was a teenager. Howard was accidental, something that started when both he and Betty weren't thinking of the future, but were wrapped up in the moment, after school on Betty's parents little couch before her dad got home from the day shift. It was her first time. She'd admitted it. His too, if truth be told. Two kids, fumbling around, playing with this new magic. They surely weren't thinking how it might change everything.

He'd only seen baby Howard once, when he had been a few weeks old. He'd waited until there was no car parked in the driveway of Betty's parents house. He'd knocked on the door and Betty opened it. She looked surprised to see him, but she asked him in.

'Come on,' she'd said. 'Come see what you've done.' Roy couldn't work out if she was mad or just tired. She looked a real mess, like she hadn't brushed her hair in a week, and she smelled kind of sour. They went right past the couch where it had happened all that time ago, and into a little room with closed curtains. There was a desk on one side of the room and a crib on the other, and hardly enough room for both of them. Betty reached into the crib to pick up the baby.

'Don't do that,' he said, but she picked it up anyway and it made sputtery sounds. It seemed creepy, not like a human being.

'Do you want to hold little Howard?'

'No,' he said. It came out too loud, and Betty shushed him as she gently pushed the baby toward his chest so that he had to take it. He'd held it, and it was the strangest thing. It felt real and unreal at the same time. He didn't know what he was supposed to feel. It started making snuffling noises, and Roy said, 'Take it back.' He didn't know why the baby made him feel panicky, but he couldn't wait to get out of the room, back into the daylight. Betty lifted it away and put it back in the crib, as if handling a baby was a natural thing for her. Roy was out in the hall before Betty finished tucking it back in its bed.

'I can't believe you don't want to hold him. Your own son.' Her voice sounded sad.

'I just wanted to tell you what I'm planning to do. I've enlisted in the Navy. I'll be off next week.'

'Roy, why don't you wait a year? You're this close to graduating. You'd be crazy to leave now. I'd do anything to stay in school and finish if I could.'

'What's done is done, Bet. I can't un-enlist. I just wanted to tell you. And I'm sorry this all happened to you.' He couldn't think of what to say. He wished he hadn't come over. He'd been able to put it all out of his mind most of the time. He felt bad that he hadn't bothered to see her since she'd had to leave school, when she was getting too big to slide into the chair at her desk and the kids were all laughing and making comments. Even the teachers had seemed embarrassed.

Roy had walked out of her house that day, her strange baby-centered life, and hadn't looked back. He figured he was starting his own new world in the Navy. When he was discharged three years later he planned to go and see Betty and the boy, but he never got around to it. His mom and dad had moved to a different suburb. He could have gone back, but he didn't. He didn't make much effort to contact his high school friends, either. He saw a few old buddies now and then, but he always came away from a night at a bar with the high school guys feeling more alone than he had felt before he went out. Faded strings—barely threads now.

Fourteen years after the baby was born, Roy had bumped into an old friend of Betty's at the A&P. He wanted to ask about Betty. He thought about her from time to time. Lately, he'd begun to wonder about the boy, Howard; wondered if he looked like a younger version of himself. He remembered feeling clumsy at that age. Then, as if this woman was reading his mind, she told him Betty was living on Island Lake, out near Brighton.

'Thought you'd like to know,' she said. He wondered just what the woman had been told. He'd pretty much blocked out those months around when the baby had been born. He remembered telling a few people that he hadn't been the only guy Betty had fooled around with. He didn't know if she told her parents that he was the father, but they never came to see him or talk to his folks. For months he'd waited, planning to deny everything. She may have told her friends, though she'd sworn she hadn't.

This friend of Betty's looked pretty much out of shape for a thirty-something. Still, Roy said it was good to see her. That's what you're supposed to say. The next day he got a map of the Brighton area to see what it looked like. There were dozens of lakes dotted around the town. He drove out and found Island Lake, just off Grand River, a couple of miles east of Brighton. There were houses dotted around the edges, and a public beach and campsite. He went to the campsite and sat at an old picnic table near the recreation ground. No one else was around. He could feel a physical aching, but didn't know where to shoot it out to reach the boy. He sat there until dusk.

Within a week he had found a house for rent on the lake. Lucky, he thought, or maybe it was fate. There had been some sort of tragedy in the family, and the old couple that had owned the house sold it to a company that rented vacation homes on lakes in the area. When Roy said he wanted to move in as soon as possible the renting company was overjoyed. They gave him a good rate for a one-year agreement. He quit his job with the construction company and found another in Brighton. It all happened quickly, as if it was meant to be.

He'd moved his things in by late afternoon, and then watched as storm clouds started rolling in, at 5.30 or so. He looked from house to house, knowing somewhere his son was probably sitting down to supper, or maybe tossing around a football with friends as the light was failing. The lake was a mile and a half across at the farthest point. He had some old binoculars and had made sure he remembered which box they were packed in. Black clouds were billowing up. He scanned the houses, but no one was outside except for an old man fishing from the end of a dock nearby and someone working in her yard, securing something under a sheet of canvas. He'd been told there was a lagoon. Some of the oldest houses on the lake circled it, but everything seemed to blend together in the failing light, even with the binoculars.

He wished he had asked that woman what Betty's last name was now. He hadn't found anyone around Brighton named Kaminski when he'd looked in the phone book. He didn't have much money left, but he decided he'd need to buy a little boat with an outboard motor so he could skirt around the edges of the lake until he found them. He was thinking he'd just have to be patient when the first crack of thunder boomed so loud it made him jump. He quickly closed all the doors and the windows just as the rain began slanting down. The lake looked grey and fuzzy, like a different place. He couldn't see to the other side anymore. He could feel the same terror he always felt during storms.

There were some things that you felt that just didn't make sense. He could remember as a boy he used to go somewhere to hide when there was a storm. His mother would leave him be, and he would go to the coat closet where it was too dark to see the lightning, and the thunder was that bit quieter as he hummed songs to himself. He could bury himself among the winter coats, and sometimes he could make himself fall into a deep sleep. If his dad was home he would pull Roy out and make him sit on the couch in the living room. It would blaze with the flashing light.

Now, on the lake, he felt the old terror with each flash of lightning. The thunder seemed to roll around the lake, worse than any storm he had experienced in the city. It was as if it was a living thing. He thought of the monsters he'd seen at the movies as a boy. Back then he'd been scared, but he always knew they weren't real. He'd laugh about them afterwards. But this was real. He found himself walking from room to room, the two small bedrooms, the kitchen, the screened in porch, trying to find a place to settle until the storm was over. Had it been a mistake to rent this house? He reminded himself why he was here. If his boy was with him, he'd have to be in control. He imagined this boy, Howard, in the room with him. They'd sit at the dining room table, and Roy would reassure him.

'It's alright, Howard. There's nothing to be afraid of. I'm here.' He could almost see the electricity sizzle through the strong wire that led out toward his son.

Breathing
Early Summer 1966

The lake was so peaceful at this time of morning. He didn't dare make a sound. One look from his father would be enough to say, 'You're too young, Joe. You can't come fishing at dawn until you're old enough to just sit patiently. I won't have you ruin it for me and your Uncle Jim.'

But this morning, at just four o'clock, he'd felt his dad's hand gently shake him awake. He had been so excited, he'd hardly been able to eat the slice of toast and drink the orange juice. Then, the wonderful smell of the mosquito repellent. His mom said the smell made her sick, but he loved it. It was all part of the magic.

Out on the lake, as Uncle Jim rowed slowly and purposefully through the still water, he listened to the first birds—the ones you didn't hear later in the day. And crickets, the constant scratchy hum as they went about their lives, doing just what crickets do.

Once they had dropped the anchor and put their lines out, he didn't have to work so hard to contain himself. Just being there with his dad and uncle gave him a kind of quiet pleasure he had never felt before.

When he was little, he had wondered why they would go out so early. No attraction could pull him from his bed when it was barely light. But now, he was proud to be part of this grown up thing, taking the place that his teenage cousin Richard had held up to a few years ago.

The slight chill in the air was slowly giving way to the warmth of the sun. He looked over to the lagoon where the last mist of dawn still breathed over the water. Up until last summer he had been afraid of the lagoon, with the huge weeping willows all along the shore, bending their ropey branches right down to the black mirror of water. And under the water, weeds so thick he was sure that creatures could crawl right out over them into his boat. He would take Grandpa's old rowboat out day after day, rowing in and out of the lagoon, trying to build up his confidence, trying to conquer his fear. Each day he would row a bit further in, distracting himself by counting the waxy yellow flowers on the water lilies, wondering what could be lurking under the clusters of lily pads. The lively imagination that was good company most of the time would turn into such an inventive beast on these trips. He wished he could leave it on land as he pushed the boat off and balanced his way to the centre seat and oars, as he left behind the shouting and anger that went on between Uncle Jim and Richard.

That was last summer. This year the lagoon held no terrors. When his Grandma asked him, 'No trips to the lagoon this year, Joe?' he just shook his head. He felt pleased that he had outgrown that fear, and relieved that he had never told anyone about it in the first place. He had coped with it on his own.

The sun was rising over the tops of the trees on the east side of the lake, and still, not so much as a nibble for anyone. Joe was thinking of tomorrow, when the rest of the cousins would arrive at his grandparents' cottage. His Aunt Susie's girls, both in their teens, didn't seem to enjoy Sundays with the family. They always looked bored or cross, and he thought the lake was wasted on them. But the twins, Uncle Ned and Aunt Katie's boys, were just two years younger than Joe, and he knew they looked up to him. He could always make the rules, be in charge with them. That gave him a good, important feeling. He had felt the same sort of awe and respect for his cousin Richard, and though there was almost six years between them, Richard had always been patient and kind. Joe's mom said that even with the age difference they had a lot in common, each being an only child. But it was more than that. For as long as he could remember Richard had told him stories. When Joe was really young the stories were about him, how Joe slew the dragon and saved the world, or how Joe led his army into battle against the enemy. They were always stories that made him feel good about himself. As he grew older the stories changed. Richard would tell him about the people he learned about in his schoolbooks. He had no time for sports or friends, but he couldn't get enough of the people he called the 'giants of history', and he made these people come alive for Joe. Uncle Jim was always saying that Richard kept his nose in a book, and it wasn't healthy—wasn't natural.

The gentle floating, drifting of Joe's thoughts stopped abruptly. He could feel nibbling on his line. At first it was just a tickling sensation in his hands that he thought he must have imagined. Then, a definite little tug tug tug. He felt sort of out of breath, trying to stay calm. The fish was playing with the bait.

Come on, he thought. Take it. Don't play it safe. Eat the juicy worm.

Dad and Uncle Jim were aware of the drama.

'That-a-boy!' they whispered. 'Stay calm, wait until he takes the bait. Now reel him in. Steady, steady. Nice goin' Joe, the first fish of the morning!'

As Joe pulled the fish from the water, Uncle Jim made his way to him, caught the fish, a long slender bass, in the net. He removed the hook from its mouth, and slid it into the red plastic bucket wedged in the front of the boat.

'A bass, Joe! He must be ten inches long! Now, I guess he'd appreciate a bit of lake in the bucket with him.'

Uncle Jim bailed half a dozen big mugs of water into the bucket, and the fish, with its real/unreal eye, stopped its frantic flapping, and started to try to swim. Another few mugs worth and it circled around and around, looking for the way out of its hopeless new world.

Joe couldn't believe it. The first one to catch a fish this morning. He felt strong and powerful, but had to work hard to keep from looking at the fish. With each flash around the bucket, Joe was aware of its panic. Grandpa had always said: 'God put the fish in this lake just for us.' The old man used to laugh as Joe would watch with disgust mixed with fascination as the old hands scraped the scales from the piles of fish, cut their heads off, then deftly gutted them using the old knife with the little horn handle.

'My sons aren't raising two sissies, are they? God above!'

Joe made himself sit through the whole ritual until all the fish were stacked on the enamel plate and the mound of heads and bloody mess was wrapped in newspaper, ready to be burned with the other garbage. He had stopped thinking about the fish that would no longer swim in the mysterious deep water of the lake. He was thinking of Richard.

As he watched the fish now—*his* fish—he thought of Richard again. He remembered one day a year ago. Richard had taken him out in the rowboat. Joe was expecting him to tell one of his histories as he rowed quickly and smoothly across the lake. Instead, he started talking about 'this boy'.

'There's this boy, Joe. And he doesn't fit in anywhere. Not with his family, and not at school, either. He's tried hard to be what people want him to be, but he just can't.'

Then he stopped talking. Joe leaned over a bit so his fingers could reach the water. He waited for Richard to start talking again, as he watched his fingers divide the water for a brief second, and then leave a little wake behind. He had the idea Richard might be talking about himself, but he wasn't sure, and he didn't know what to say. He watched the oars dip in the water again and again until they returned to shore in front of their grandparent's cottage.

At the end of last summer, when Richard was fifteen, he had run away. And now Joe realized that Richard had felt that coping with the unknown world would be easier than trying to grow into the man his father expected him to be. And easier than facing the tough macho boys at school who called him queer and spread filthy stories about him. He had run away and left everything he knew.

No one had heard from him in the ten months that he had been gone. And no one talked about him. At first Joe thought it was because everyone was so angry with Richard. Once he'd tried to make it a bit better by reminding them of the times Richard had taken him for long walks around the lake. But everyone's faces had told him to stop. Aunt Ruth had left the room in tears, and Uncle Jim had looked him right in the eye, helpless and hurt, not looking grown-up at all. He'd glanced over to his dad, who just shook his head. Joe knew he couldn't fill up this emptiness, so he had left it alone and gone out to stare across the lake.

And now, Joe could feel his Uncle Jim's eyes on him as he watched the fish in the bucket. It was less frantic now. Was it starting to give up? Wasn't there enough oxygen left for him in the gallon or so of water? Joe braced his feet on the bottom of the boat and pulled the bucket from where it was wedged. Then, without a word, he poured the water and the fish back into the lake. He didn't look at his dad at the far end of the boat. His Uncle Jim nodded to him to haul up the anchor. Then, with the long wet line and anchor safely in the boat, Joe watched as Uncle Jim began rowing to shore.

Mother's Daughter
Early Summer 1966

When I was little everyone said I looked just like my mother. We'd visit her family in North Carolina, and they would always fuss in that southern way, 'Kathy, you're the image of your mama at this age. It's like having her as a child all over again.' It's not surprising they thought that. They'd get out boxes of pictures, old black and white ones with wavy edges, and there she'd be, staring straight into the camera, her short dark hair like a clumsy helmet. The look in her eye seemed to challenge, as if to say 'you can't capture me'. Then we would return home, and I'd wander through the family photo album to find myself, or the person I had been not so long ago, in the same shapeless little dresses, the same sad hairdo. But the defiance wasn't there. Instead, I looked timid, almost afraid. I still hate to have my photo taken.

There is no photographic record of my first day at school, but I can see it in my mind, running like a home movie. Mama, my sister and I are walking down our street toward the big school building. I am almost five. Laurie skips ahead, happy and carefree. She's done this every day for three years, and wants me to see how advanced, how superior she is. Mama is holding my hand, and I'm walking along with her, but I feel as though I'm being dragged, pulled from my safe world of home, my Raggedy Anne doll, the big green rocking chair, and the constant comforting voice of the kitchen radio, filling in the background with songs of twilight-time and all-I-have-to-do-is-dream. My camera didn't record anything at school, but I remember the feeling I took away with me. It was as if everyone knew each other already, and I had just been sent to watch.

I've always been a watcher. To be honest, it's a way of taking without giving. I know the children who are more outgoing, more aggressive, may appear greedy, but they are the ones who earn what they get, with the occasional bruise or injured pride along the way.

Is curiosity a bad thing? Is it something to be washed away, or at least kept politely hidden? And where do you draw the line between a healthy interest in other people and being just plain nosy?

Now that I'm ten, we don't go down to North Carolina much. I'm spending the long, hot summer with my grandma at her cottage on a lake. She lives about an hour from the city, so my parents work during the week and come out to the lake most weekends.

Part of what makes summer wonderful here is in my grandma herself. She is always asking questions, and makes me feel as if I am the most important, interesting person she knows. Mama never asks questions. I figured she has been so convinced that I am just a little replica of her, she is sure she knows every thought that goes through my head.

Next door to Grandma's house is Surf Side Lodge, a huge hodgepodge of a building that contains about eight apartments. People come here to vacation for a week or two, to get away from the city heat and enjoy the swimming, boating and fishing. I am friends with Janice, the owner's daughter. She is a bland blonde girl. Our friendship is quiet and kind of boring. Most of the kids live on the other side of the lake. We share out time between my grandma's quiet little beach and dock, and the long grand beach and playground of Surf Side Lodge. Janice chats with the more friendly of the guests, and I tag along.

On Monday morning Janice mentioned that there was a blind man called Bill staying at the lodge. I tried to imagine how someone who couldn't see would enjoy a vacation at a lake. It seems sad that he wouldn't be able to see the sparkling blue surface in the sunlight, with its big island and little island poking out of the water about a mile from our beach.

At the far corner, a railroad track runs only yards from the shore. Every hour or so long sleek silver passenger trains pass, and sometimes in between there are even longer freight trains, rusty red cars and yellow cars going on and on. If the train is going slowly, I always stop what I'm doing to count the cars. I usually lose track before the last one, the little red caboose passes from sight, pulling the train's wailing whistle away with it. The blind man could hear the train's signal, and the motorboats, and the children splashing in the water. I wondered if he would venture in.

Later that morning, I had gone for a swim. I'd closed my eyes and walked out to the deeper water, but I felt kind of dizzy very quickly. And when I tried floating on my back with my eyes still closed the sensation of having my ears dipping in and out of the water confused the sounds around me. It made me feel panicky. The world seemed too strange. I decided no sightless person could get any joy from a dip in the lake. I dried myself off, and walked over to find Janice. She was sitting at a picnic table, watching a man and woman playing cards.

The lady said they had heard music coming across the lake until midnight the night before. She asked Janice if she knew where it had come from.

'That's the Blue Lantern dancehall. It's that white building, over there on the other side of the lake. At night they have live bands, and they light it up outside so it looks blue and reflects in the water.'

The man smiled, and fingered the corner of the card he had just drawn. I realized that he must be Bill. I was pleased that he seemed happy enough to be sitting outside under the big elm trees playing cards.

Then I remembered that I'd promised Grandma to be back by 12.30 for lunch. She hated to have to call or search for me.

I asked the lady if she knew the time. The man lifted his wrist and flipped a little cover off the face of his watch, ran his fingers over it quickly, and said, 'It's twenty past twelve.'

I thanked him, and told Janice I'd meet her at her apartment later in the afternoon.

As I sat with my grandma eating sandwiches and salad I told her about something I'd seen that morning before I had my swim. Some children who were staying at the Lodge had built an elaborate sandcastle. They had decorated it with the little spiral shells of water-snails. I was about to come and get Grandma to see it, but then another guest had caught a catfish. It had swallowed the hook and because the man had been afraid to try to grasp the fleshy black thing in case he got stung by one of its 'whiskers', he had cut the line, sinker and all, and let it swim away. In the meantime, a toddler had run back and forth over the sandcastle until it was a damp lump on the beach.

I had been expecting Grandma to say how sorry she was that the castle was ruined but instead she sat drumming her fingers on the table. She shook her head.

'That was a cruel and cowardly thing to do, Kathy,' she said. When it was obvious that I didn't understand what she meant she continued.

'That fish will have a long, slow death. Did that man think it ceased to exist once it was back in the lake?'

She pushed her chair from the table and carried our plates to the sink. I knew I'd have to spend some time working out why it was okay to catch the fish and eat them, which Grandma did quite happily, but to make them suffer and die for no reason was wrong.

While Grandma was washing the dishes and I dried, I told her about Bill, about his watch and the playing cards with the little holes punched in the corners so that he could 'read' what they were with his fingers.

A little later in the afternoon I walked back to Janice's apartment.

'You'll never guess what, Kathy. Bill is having a piano delivered this afternoon. He told my dad he just couldn't bear two weeks without it. Dad asked the other guests, and no-one seems to mind.'

As soon as the piano was delivered Bill started playing, songs I knew from the radio and ones I didn't, one after another with hardly a pause in-between. We could hear them on the beach, and in the playground. I was sure Grandma could hear through her open windows. Soon it seemed as if something was missing when he would stop playing for a while. People would call at his window, asking for favorite songs, and the chords would just roll out of him, through the piano.

Sometimes he'd stop for a while and play cards outside, or be taken for rides in row-boats or outboard motor-boats, and once I saw him standing knee deep in the lake, with his companion at his side. One of the other guests called to him from the shore.

'What are you doing in the lake, Bill? Your piano is waiting.'

He leaned over until his fingers touched the water and ran his hand back and forth slowly a few times. Then he turned and walked out of the water, and back to his apartment, a big smile on his face.

In the evenings Grandma and I would sit at the kitchen table playing canasta, and listening to Bill's piano.

I remember that whole week as a magical time. No one felt the need to keep to themselves. Even a young honeymooning couple joined in. There were huge barbecues, horseshoe tournaments, and swimming races for the children, all organized by the guests themselves. On

Saturday, as night began to fall and the crickets started their own song, Bill went up to his apartment and began playing the piano. One or two people followed him up. Then, in twos or threes, the other guests went along. I asked my grandma if I could go, too.

She could hear the piano and people singing. She walked me over, but declined the invitation to stay. When I went inside, I was amazed at how many people had squeezed into the tiny apartment. Other than two families who had gone into town for dinner and a movie, everyone was there. I watched the people's faces as they joined in. Some looked a bit shy, like singing in public was embarrassing. Others obviously didn't even think about what they were doing. The music they were making seemed natural to them; they were having a great time. After a while I was singing too, remembering songs from my mama's radio, and just being swept along with the other voices.

Then we were singing a song that I knew and loved, though I didn't really understand. It always made me feel sad and happy at the same time. We hadn't been singing long when I realized a few people were just listening. Then a few more stopped singing. Bill kept playing quietly, so I continued. I was aware that there were only two voices, another little girl's and mine singing the words of Hi-Lili, Hi Lo; the sadness of love...

When the song was over, we sang another, and then another. But it took some time for the thrill inside me to calm down. I felt proud, as if I was a small part of something huge and wonderful. I was suddenly older and richer, and a bit special.

After a while the people with children started filtering away and I knew I should be going, too. I said goodnight to Bill, and one of the adults took me back home to Grandma's.

*

The next day my parents came. I told them about Bill and his piano, and the singsong, and the way everyone was so friendly. I told them how Bill could play any song you asked for, and how he had a special watch, and only went in the lake once.

When my dad's brother and his family arrived I went off with my cousins for a swim. As usual my dad and my uncle went fishing in the boat, and Mama, Grandma, and my aunt just sat at the kitchen table talking all afternoon. Bill must have gone out with his companion, because we didn't hear the piano all day. I had been looking forward to Mama hearing him play.

We had a big fish fry that night. As usual, when the meal was over, and the dishes were washed and put away, my dad and Uncle Scott started getting ready for the drive back to the city.

Mama took me into the living room by myself.

'I don't want you going over to Surf Side Lodge this week. I know you. You're just curious about that poor blind man. Heavens knows what kind of person you'll grow into if you don't learn to mind your own business.'

She had waited for the last minute before leaving so there would be no chance of an argument. She had told Grandma that I was to stay away, and though I could tell Grandma didn't agree I also knew she wouldn't go against Mama's wishes. I could see that Grandma was upset, but I was too wrapped up in my own hurt and anger to work out why Grandma didn't tell Mama she was wrong.

The next morning when Janice came over to play I sent her away, saying I wanted to spend the week with my Grandma and didn't want to play with her any more.

And mid-morning, when I heard Bill begin to play something sweet and gentle, I asked Grandma to close the windows.

'No, Kathy. It's too hot to do that. Besides, I think you know that's not the way to cope with this.'

I knew neither of us could change my mother's ready-made idea of me. I hoped that my memory picture of that special evening was safely stored, proof of what could be. I went to my bedroom, closed the door, and sat on the floor with my hands over my ears to stop any trace of sound from the outside world. Then I retreated to a safe, untrespassable place in my mind.

Brothers
Summer 1966

It's James and John. Always has been. I used to think, why does James get to be first? Will I always be second? Mom says, 'James comes first because he was born before you. He's fourteen minutes older. So it's James and John.' It's strange to think he had a head start, especially when you think what's happening to him now.

We didn't get here until after dark. Dad had complications at work, and then all of Detroit was one big traffic jam. When we got out in the country, Dad got lost, and Mom was upset because James was going to get overtired. But then he fell asleep, so it was okay, except it was boring, being in the back seat on my own. All I could see from my window was the dark rushing by. The lake was just a big stretch of darkness, too, with lights in some houses around the edges. And I could smell a barbeque somewhere, even though it was late. The crickets sounded the same as at home; one constant scratchy song, all night long.

The house is okay. It's more like a little log cabin; the walls are just stacks of tree trunks on the outside, like the house where ole Abe Lincoln grew up. Dad says, 'Basic, but good enough for a month in high summer. The pillows smell musty—Mom's word. She says we'll put them out in the sunshine in the morning and they'll freshen up. I can't wait until tomorrow, to see the lake. I've tried to see it in my imagination, but I can't. James and I used to talk in bed. Now he just falls straight to sleep, and I talk to myself in my head. And sometimes I listen to him breathing... breathing.

It's early. The lake is amazing. It stretches a couple miles, and it's black and still, like a giant mirror. The trees by the edge, huge weeping willows, reach right into the water and then turn upside down, as if they are reaching for themselves. There's a bit of mist on the far side of the lake, hovering, like a big sprawling ghost. I wonder if the fish can see the mist, if they ever look up. Their whole world is the lake. I've seen them jumping. I've counted five so far this morning, but most of the time I'm looking in the wrong place, and only see them from the corner of my eye. It seems as if the lake pulls them back in. I wonder if they're catching bugs, or if they like to feel air as much as we like to swim. The crickets have stopped but I can hear some other insects hissing.

I wish James would wake up. Mom said he'll be able to sit out after breakfast if he's not feeling too tired. The water's cool and soft. It's turning bluer as the sun climbs up the sky. I don't see why James couldn't come wading a little bit. The mist is going, and it's getting hot already.

Dad was mad when he got up and checked on James, and saw that I wasn't in bed. He said I shouldn't have snuck out. It didn't feel like I was sneaking. I just couldn't wait. He's gone for an early morning swim, while it's quiet. His shoulders look big and powerful, from all the lifting he does at work, I guess. He's a no nonsense swimmer, back and forth, like there's no fun to it, like it's something he just has to do.

It's almost ten, and James just got up. He used to be the one who got up early, and I'd stay in bed, writing stories in my head. Now Mom has him under a blanket and a beach umbrella. At least she put the sun lounger on the beach, a few feet from shore. He's kicked off the blanket, and wants me to tell him a story. I need to think *fish*.

It's just a normal morning, and I'm swimming through a forest of lake weed in the deep dark water. I'm a pike, about eight inches long, minding my own business, browsing along the bottom. This is big fish territory. I shouldn't be here. I feel a surge run through the water. Something is coming toward me, menacing! A huge fish? There's no time to bend my body around to look. I sprint through the weeds, around their thick bases. Is the big fish slowing down, or can it just plow through? Now I'm swimming up toward the lake-top. Surely the big fish isn't behind me now. I'm safe again. I can feel it. I skim along the upper edge of my world, where the warm water feels light as it flows through my gills. I hear a noise coming from somewhere far away. I flick my tail, and do a little fish dance. I like the way it feels. There's that noise again.

'Fi--ish! Oh, fi--ish!' James calls, and his voice skims out across the water, and we laugh. I'll work on the story, and maybe tell it to him again later, if he wants. He didn't use to listen to my stories much. He was too busy. Dad always used to say James was the doer and I was the dreamer. . .

I'll need to think more about the lake, and the fish. Maybe my stories are silly. Maybe fish don't think. Maybe they're doers. Maybe the dreaming fish would have been eaten by now.

I was so tired last night; I couldn't even stay awake to make sure James got to sleep. While he napped yesterday, I spent the whole time in the lake. I tried swimming along the bottom so I could see what the fish see. I had to fight to stay down there—my body kept coming up to the surface, like the lake was trying to spit me out. My eyes got all bloodshot, plus my shoulders and the back of my neck got sunburned. Mom says she's not going to let me swim today. I'll have to spend the high-sun hours in the shade with James, but that's okay. I've had a good idea for a story to tell him.

Imagine being a fish, with eyes on each side of your head, and no arms and legs. Just floppy fins and scales like chainmail. Imagine being a tiny minnow, swimming along with a hundred of your brothers and sisters, and everyone turns left together and swims along, and—oops!—everyone darts to the right. It's like a big dance, made up of thin squiggles of fish.

I remember when I was just a minnow, and there were so many of us, always together. Then, there seemed to be less and less. The bigger we grew, the fewer of us there were. No one ever stopped and looked back to see what we were swimming away from.

And now I swim alone. Sometimes I see another pike about the same size as me, and I wonder if he's a brother fish, but we both just swim off in different directions. It's lonely being a fish.

'Poor lonely fish,' James laughs. He laughs at all my stories, and that's a good thing, even though part of me is hurt that he can't begin to imagine a fish having feelings. But surely they must, or they wouldn't swim away from danger.

We sit in the shade of the huge striped umbrella and watch the lake together. James says, 'There are fourteen boats out there right now: three big cabin cruisers; four littler motor boats; a big pontoon thing, that's not a boat at all, really; two little sail boats; and the rest are just row boats. Fourteen.'

He's always liked to count things.

'Which would you like to be in right now?' I ask.

'Oh, one of the little speed boats, of course. But it wouldn't be any fun unless I was strong again.'

The thought that I always push away comes back to me. It's not fair that James is sick. It should be me. It wouldn't matter as much if it were me. I'm sure everyone must think it when they see how skinny he is now. It's this big unsaid thing that's always hanging in the air.

'Maybe Dad will buy one, later in the summer,' I say.

'You're dreaming again, John.'

We hear a sharp squealing coming from a few houses along the lake shore. There are three kids, our age or a little younger. They're running down a long dock and jumping into the lake. We watch as they do it over and over again. It's a girl in a blue swimsuit that squeals every time, and the noise stops each time she hits the water with a big slapping splash. It's odd, watching these kids. Last year, we'd have been like them, except we would never squeal. James would want to race, knowing he'd be sure to beat me. Then we'd float on our backs. We'd look up at the sky and talk, with the lake lapping in our ears and the sun blazing down.

James is looking out across the water. I can't see what he's locked on to. There are little glints on the waves, like tiny sparks. The pontoon boat is chugging along into view. It's so close to the shore, you can hear voices. There are four people on it, sitting at a little table in the middle, like they're in a diner. There's a white haired woman, with a beach towel over her shoulders. She throws her head back and laughs, an ugly, animal sound.

'What's she think is so funny?' James says. His voice has that sleepy sound he had when he was in the hospital the time before last—no emotion—like he doesn't really care about anything.

'I don't know,' I say. 'I'm on vacation. I don't 'do' people. Just fish.'

He sends a little smile back to me, and closes his eyes.

'You need a nap between naps?' I ask.

'No. Tell me another pike story.'

I haven't been trying to think up a story. My mind won't go to the right place.

'You just had one,' I tell him. He's drifting off to sleep anyway. I get up and walk to the edge of the lake, up to my knees, and scoop up handfuls of the cold water and splash my face and my shoulders. Then I walk up to the house. I'm brushing the wet sand off my feet outside the door and I can hear Mom inside, crying. I hear Dad's voice, but can't make out what he's saying to her. Mom never lets us see her cry. More than once this past year she's started, and she just gets up and walks out of the room in the middle of whatever's happening. When she comes back, she's got her fake smile on—the one she only used to use for strangers.

I turn around and walk back to the lake, and wade in slowly, until I'm trudging hard against the water, and it's getting too deep to walk. I start to swim. I'm swimming straight out, into the deep water, through tangles of weeds, through clearer water. I try to think of the fish, my pike, swimming under me, but the water feels empty. I swim until my arms start to ache, and I can't swim anymore. I turn around and look at our vacation house. I doggy-paddle for a moment. James and his umbrella are just a speck on the beach. I turn over on my back and start floating, catching my breath. I can stroke almost silently with my arms.

We're going home in the morning. Mom says we're too far from the hospital here. She says it makes her nervous, and it's not good for James. It makes him exhausted. I wonder if she feels bad for him, having the lake and not being able to have any fun in it. We've come to bed early, because he's so tired. Mom says she doesn't want to hear me talking, keeping him awake.

'I've got a story for you, John,' James says. 'If I was a fish, I'd just swim away. I'd find the source of the lake, and swim into it, like the salmon on TV that swim upstream. I'd swim and fight my way from here and never look back. I'd just get out.'

I listen to James breathing, little fast breaths. They take forever to slow down, for him to finally fall asleep. I try to think of some story to take me away from here, but my mind is blank. There's nothing.

Grandma Says
Summer 1966

Grandma says if I spend a lot of time rowing around the lake, one day I'll have big boobies like her. I come out every day after breakfast, before it gets too hot. The lifejacket is heavy and sticky, but Grandma would kill me if I didn't wear it. Grandpa's binoculars are always on a hook next to the front door, and she keeps an eye on me even when I'm half way around, along the edge of the lake.

I row out until the sandy bottom starts to get weedy. Then, when I can't see the bottom or the little fish anymore I turn and start rowing in a big half-circle around half the lake. Just half around takes me most of the morning. Here, where there aren't many houses or people, I can sing, or talk to myself, to practice conversations I'll have when I'm a teenager, like my cousin Marianne. She has boyfriends, and goes dancing at the Blue Lantern. I can hear the music from it on Friday nights. It comes over the lake when the water is black. All kinds of exiting things happen wherever Marianne is.

I can splash with the oars, back and forth, or go around and around by just using one oar. I have to be especially brave when I row anywhere near what Mama calls the 'shabby house,' where that teenage boy lives. He shouted at me once to get out of his part of the lake, even though the lake belongs to everybody. There's no swimming in front of his house, because the water is mucky right up to the shore, and the weeds grow thick up to the surface. It makes me terrified. I'm sure things could crawl out over them and right into the boat; things like the muskrats that live in front of the big empty house or, worse than that, the snapping turtles. I'm most afraid of them. When we're swimming, and can see their heads poking out of the water a long way off, we always get out, just in case they decide to come and have a look at who's swimming in their lake.

Once last summer Grandpa caught a big snapper when he was fishing from the shore. He reeled it in, and put it in the rowboat without breaking his line. He left it there all day and night, 'til it got exhausted from trying to find the way out. Then he took it out, and put it on the steps between the sand and Grandma's yard. He put his foot on its hard shell, and pulled the line so its head poked out, and smashed its head with a hammer.

When Grandpa died just after Christmas it was the first funeral I ever went to. It wasn't at all like I imagined it would be. For the service in the church I was in the front row with Momma, Daddy and Grandma. There were prayers, and then someone went up to the pulpit and talked about Grandpa, what a fine man he was and all the good things he had done in a war. When the man finished everyone started to sing Grandpa's favorite hymn. The singing was loud because there were so many people in the church. Daddy looked straight ahead and didn't sing, but tears were running down his face. I didn't know men could cry. The music from the organ felt like it was shaking right through me.

I looked at the big grey casket, and tried to make myself believe Grandpa was really in there. But all I could see in my mind was the ugly look on his face when he killed the turtle, and the turtle being alive and then dead, and I started to cry.

Momma sat down on the pew so she was as tall as me, and held my face in her hands. She said, just loud enough for me to hear over the singing, 'It's okay, sweetie, Grandpa's in heaven now.'

Sally Ann Maybe
Summer 1966

Dear Diary,

Life is weird, and it just keeps getting weirder. You could write a book about this place. Maybe, when I'm grown up and people start taking me seriously, maybe I will. My dad says the weird around here is all very small scale. He says, 'Sally Ann, if you think this is weird, you just wait.'

So, the weird stuff: There's a man who goes around the lake in a little motor boat, one hand steering and the other holding binoculars to his eyes. He must be the world's biggest snoop. I've seen him three times. I told my mom and she called him bold. She told my sister and me to come inside if we see him. She says maybe he likes looking at girls in swimsuits, and that's not nice. I thought about mentioning all the girls in swimsuits in the Miss America contest. I know my dad likes to watch that, so I can't imagine what could be wrong about looking at a seven year old and an eleven year old. Mom always says I ask too many questions.

More weird stuff: There was a family that came to stay in the log cabin, and they only stayed for two nights. And one of the boys stayed all wrapped up on the beach like a little old lady.

The weirdest thing was dad's cousin and her friend came to visit last Saturday. Mom made the four of us kids sit at the kitchen table and she explained that Mary is a nun. None (ha ha) of us are Catholic, least of all my dad. She said we should be on our best behaviour, and we weren't to ask nosy questions, and she gave me the evil eye when she said it.

So on Saturday late morning they arrived. They wore long black dresses and head veils that swung down past their elbows. They had stiff white around their faces and necks. It looked like card it was so starchy. Mary never stopped smiling. We had lunch, and Mary and Sister Martha ate like normal people except for the stiff things around their necks. Mary had little beads of sweat on her forehead and nose. They insisted on washing the dishes. Then all the grown ups sat in the screened porch and talked. It was too hot for them to sit on the outside. I could see that both Mary and Sister Martha were just about to melt in their big black dresses.

When mom went to make lemonade I sat next to Mary. I wanted to ask lots of questions, like what it was like being married to Jesus. (They both had wedding rings on their right hands), and what do nuns do for fun, but I knew mom would think I was being nosy. Mary said why wasn't I swimming with the other kids. I explained that since I was the oldest and found their behaviour childish, I only went in to have a swim every day at four o'clock.

It's wonderful, I told them. I just swim and float on my back, and maybe do summersaults and hand stands under the water. Then I thought how maybe Mary and Sister Martha wanted to swim but couldn't because they didn't have swim-suits. I said they could both borrow suits from my mom. It was hard to tell what shape they were under their dresses, but mom has a whole drawer full, and we've never had a guest yet that she couldn't find one for. They both just laughed and Mary fiddled with the long white cord that hung from her waist.The water is so cool and lovely I said, and Dad keeps the weeds cleared so the bottom is sandy. I told them I was absolutely sure that they'd love it. Then Mom came back with the lemonade and told me to hush up.

They were supposed to go back to their sacred heart house in the city at seven, but when they went out to start their car it just went a few feet and stopped dead. They came back in and were on the phone for a long time. Mary said they would need to stay the night if that was okay. I said they could use my room. Imagine having a nun sleep in your own bed. So Mom changed the sheets and made up the roll away bed in my room. They went to bed early. Mary said they had a lot of prayers to say. I stood by the door thinking maybe I could hear them but I couldn't hear a thing.

Everyone went to bed pretty early. I got to sleep in the screened porch and listened to the crickets until I fell asleep. For some reason I woke up. It must have been after midnight. There were almost no lights on in any of the houses around the lake, but the moon was full. It shined a white streak of light across the water. I could hear some little splashes. I heard a giggle, and a shush. There, right in front of the house were two heads bobbing in the water. I watched them for a few minutes, and then went back to bed. They came in the side door, perfectly silently, and went back to my bedroom. I'm old enough to keep a secret.

Love,
SA

Colors
Summer 1966

5.50 a.m. The wet sand feels cool and clammy against Vincent's bare feet. Aqua, he thinks, like the Spanish word for water: agua. But no, it's never aqua. That's the color of the swimming pool in Brighton. Artificial. Trying too hard. This early, with the sun just coming up, the water is shifting from black to navy blue. Vincent thinks of himself as blue. He lets the word filter through his mind. Blue, like a sunny day, with fluffy white clouds floating over. Deep blue. Shallow blue. Blue specked with silver like waves on a lake. The muzzy blue of a sad song. The blues—that's what they call it. If he could have only one color, it would be blue. Blue could be everything. Everything could be blue.

He wonders if fish can see color, if they see the sky above their lake, the green of the lake weed. Do the little sunfish know their tiny bellies are yellow, orange, rosy red, like they're carrying around their own personal sunsets?

It feels as if the lake belongs to him this time of the morning. There are just a few men out fishing, their rowboats anchored down here and there in the stillness, and they are as still as statues, waiting for a nibble, a bite. His mom will get up at seven, will leave for work at ten to eight. When she leaves she'll ask what he plans to do with his day. And as she opens the door she will say, 'Don't go in the lake.' She worries. She acts as if he isn't careful. There are other kids who live on the lake who are left alone while their parents are out at work. Vincent is sure they get up to all kinds of stuff, but nothing bad happens to them. It's not worth arguing with his mother. Besides, he has plans for today. He's going to pull some weeds for Amanda from 2.30 till 3.30. Then she'll give him a glass of ice tea on her porch. He enjoys talking to her. Who would think you could have things to talk about with someone older than your mother? The rest of the day will be his.

Once his mother has gone he goes to his room to get the cloth bag that holds his art supplies. He has used the money he earned doing jobs for Amanda to buy the bag, charcoals, and a box of twenty-four colored pencils. On Saturday he went to the stationers to get a good quality sketchpad, but they cost too much, so he bought a big scrapbook instead. The paper isn't as thick and is pale cream instead of white, but he thinks it will be good for practice. He plans to write his ideas down on the back page. He wants to fill an entire page with drawings of trees: whole trees, then a sample leaf of each, and maybe squares of what the different barks looked like. He's been practicing tree shapes on scraps of paper for days. But now, he's thinking SQUARES.

He spreads out his art supplies on the kitchen table. He turns to the first page and draws a square of light gray in the bottom corner, less than half an inch high. It's not a perfect square, but that's okay. Perfect is boring. Next to the gray, he draws a grassy green square that seems to lean into the gray one, and then an orange one that's a bit wobbly at the top. He joins a slightly smaller purple square above, and works at spreading upwards and outwards. He works until he has almost filled the page. His fingers hurt from holding the pencils, but he likes the look of what he's done. He notices the clock. He's been working for hours and hasn't realized it's past lunchtime. He gets a glass of grape juice and comes back to the table. He doesn't have a pencil the deep purple of his grape juice. In the art supply department of the stationer's, they have a huge flat metal box of artist pencils. Once he's earned more money, he'll buy it.

He makes himself a peanut butter and jelly sandwich and wonders how you can mix colors to come up with the rich sandy brown of peanut butter. He takes a peach from the fruit bowl and turns it to look at all the different yellows and reds on the fuzzy skin. He takes a bite and inside the peach is a lush yellow, hardly peach colored at all. Well, he thinks, an orange is orange through and through. The peach is ripe; the juice runs down his hand almost to his elbow. He wipes his hands on a paper towel, puts his dish and glass in the sink, and goes outside to the end of the little dock. The water is only a few feet deep. He stretches out on his stomach and dangles his right arm over the edge. As his fingers touch the water he sees he has disturbed a school of minnows. They dart away in a few different directions, like a big swirling design. Vincent has a blue-green pencil. That's what he'll draw tomorrow, on page two of his book. He washes the rest of the peach juice from his arm and chin and walks back to the house, smiling. Surely his mother wouldn't consider he'd 'gone in the lake.'

The temperature must be over ninety. 'Blisteringly hot' Amanda had said when he arrived. She had drenched a big area of grass under her huge oak tree earlier. Since then the sun has shifted, so he is sitting in full sunshine, trying to pry dandelions out of the ground. The heat seems to spread laziness all around the lake. The leaves aren't rustling. Only one or two birds seem to have the energy to caw out from the trees. There's the soft buzz from a motorboat from the far side of the lake. Even with the earlier drenching the ground is hard. The roots are long and don't want to give up their hold on planet earth. Over and again Vincent comes up with a handful of leaves and no root. He should give up, tell Amanda he'll try again after a rain. He looks up toward the house. Amanda is busy inside. He tries another weed.

'Well, what do we have here? Hello, Spanky.' Howard stands a few feet away, the sun glowing out from behind him. If Vincent had seen him coming, walking along the shoreline, he would have been prepared. You have to be careful when you talk to Howard. You have to be nice, but not too polite, to make sure you don't make mistakes and give Howard a reason to be mean to you.

'Hi Howard. How's it going?'

'Terrific. Just terrific.' His voice sounds bored. He takes a last puff on his cigarette, walks to the oak tree and stubs it out on the bark.

'No!' Vincent says before he can stop himself. Howard lets the cigarette butt fall to the ground.

'Oh, dear. Have I done something wrong? So sorry.' He starts to pick at the bark, flicking little chunks at Vincent.

'What are you worried about? It's not your tree. What are you doing at this old bird's house anyway? Don't you have enough of your own weeds to play with?'

It hurts Vincent's eyes to look toward the sun. He feels that sick feeling he has whenever Howard singles him out.

'Just helping out,' he starts, and Amanda is on her porch.

'That's enough for today, Vincent. Come inside. I'll get you some iced tea.'

'Am I invited, too?' Howard asks, his voice innocent. 'I'm Spanky's, I mean Vincent's good buddy.'

'No, sorry,' Amanda says as she turns back to the door.

'Stupid old biddy,' Howard says under his breath. 'Oh, well. See you later,' he says to Vincent, and heads back to the beach.

Inside, Vincent sits at the kitchen table.

'We'll just wait until he has time to get back to his house, then we'll go out on the porch. He can't see us from there,' Amanda says.

Back outside, they slip into the two rocking chairs under the shade of the big green awning. They have never talked about Howard. Vincent isn't sure if she knows anything about him. He isn't mentioned again. Instead, Vincent tells her about his colored pencils, the picture he has been working on and the one he plans to start tomorrow.

'I'd be interested in seeing them. But only if you want to show me.' As they talk Vincent draws lines on the sweaty glass. Cold water drips down on his knees. The heat makes him drowsy. It's nice to sit and watch the lake, to see it from a different view. Vincent had always thought his house was at the center, the starting point. When he is out in the rowboat he is always surprised how tiny it is among the others. From some angles he can't see it at all. The big houses stand out proudly, rising up from their sea walls, their grassy sweeps of land. Howard's shabby old house must have been there a long time, and it must have looked nice once. Vincent can't imagine it. He closes his eyes for what seems like a moment, but when he opens them Amanda is standing, fishing dollar bills out of her wallet. He pulls himself to his feet.

'No, you don't need to pay me today. I didn't really do anything.'

'I've enjoyed your company,' she says as she zips the wallet closed.

'Me, too.' He's pleased that she doesn't think she needs to buy his company, but he's calculating the delay this will cause in buying the box of colored pencils.

'Before you go, Vincent, I thought you might like to borrow this book. I think it must have been my father's. I found it in the attic. It's a bit musty.'

The book has a dark green hard cover. It's not much bigger than a paperback. *Today's Art* is embossed in gold. 'Today' obviously happened many years ago. There are a lot of words, and prints of paintings by Picasso and sculptures by Henry Moore, all in black and white.

'Strange, isn't it?' Amanda says. 'I try to imagine the colors, but I can't.'

'I'll bring it back next time. Thanks.'

*

As soon as he's back in the door of his own house he starts opening windows, and turns on the big window fan to draw out the heat. Then he stops to check on his drawing from earlier in the day. He's pleased. He sets Amanda's book on its end with its pages forming a quarter circle. The pictures are frustrating but he'll spend some time trying to color them in using his imagination. Maybe he could copy some detail of one of Picasso's strange jumbles, create his own design. He remembers he hasn't opened the bedroom windows to let the breeze filter through the screens. From his mother's room he thinks he hears the slam of the kitchen door. Did he forget to lock it?

Vincent's legs feel heavy as he walks through the hall and into the living room. He slowly steps into the kitchen.

'Spanky, what would your mother think if she knew you didn't lock your screen door? She wouldn't be happy, would she? I mean, *anybody* could walk in and steal all this precious stuff.'

Howard is seated at the kitchen table, his chair pushed back. His legs look big, straining in his tight Bermuda shorts. His eyes look mean. Vincent should tell Howard to get out. He wasn't invited. Maybe he should be nice, but not too friendly, and say his mother will be home any minute. He looks at the clock. She won't be back for more than an hour. Howard wouldn't believe him anyway. Or he wouldn't care. Vincent should say something, but nothing seems right or helpful.

'You're not being very neighborly. Shouldn't you offer me some Kool-Aid or ice tea? And what's going on with you and that old lady? You're a weird one, Spanky. And you have weird friends.'

'She's just a lady who lives alone and needs a bit of help sometimes. She's nice.'

'Nice! Ha!' Howard roars a laugh, and reaches across the table to the fruit bowl. He picks up a peach, inspects it, then takes a bite, making a nasty slurping noise. He slides Vincent's scrapbook in front of him.

'Boxes, boxes, boxes,' he says. 'Boring, boring, boring.' He takes another bite of the peach and then places it in the middle of the page of squares. Vincent can see the peach juice soaking into the pages. Howard stands up.

'This lake is boring. *You* are boring, Spanky. I've got better things to do.' With one sticky finger he pushes Amanda's book over and heads for the door. As he passes he smacks Vincent on the top of the head.

Shannon
Summer 1966

The sun warms her thick brown hair. She presses her hands down on the top of her head to push the heat into her skull. She's only ten years old, but she knows this: she is pretty. She's much prettier than her older sister Frieda. No one has ever said so, but when people learn they are related they say things like 'Really? I never would have guessed.'

When they were little they played together all the time. They played with the cat from the hotel, fed her the cream from the top of the milk bottle. A couple of summers ago they saw 'Kitty' poking around behind dad's garage, coming and going all one morning. When she left the yard they went to see if they could figure out why. They found four tiny kittens, two calico and two gray. Their mom said not to touch them for the first few weeks or the mother might take them away or, worse yet, abandon them. Frieda named three of them, but she told Shannon she could name one. Shannon's kitten's name changed a few times a day. She was Fluffy, then she was Tiny, then she was Miss Donnelly (after her favorite teacher), then she was Candy Cat. Frieda said she'd have to settle on one name or the poor thing would be confused. Shannon named her Tizzy.

When the kittens were a month old the hotel owner came to their door.

'You have our cat. You have to give it back.' He didn't even know about the kittens. Their mom took the man out and showed them to him. He said he didn't want a bunch of kittens at his hotel.

The summer before that was the year of the dens. They put their mom's old pink sheet over the clotheslines and made a little daytime home, put lawn chairs inside and a blue plaid tablecloth for a rug. They had their lunches out there, cool in the pale pink light. They drank lemonade out of chipped china teacups. They brought their dolls in and put them to bed in two cardboard boxes. Frieda always told Shannon how to play.

'Now you say how nice it is to have me over for a visit. Now we can wake up our babies and give them their bottles. Remember how I showed you to wrap the doll in the blanket. No, look. Like this.' Shannon didn't mind being told. She was always happy to be carried along by Frieda's bursts of excitement.

Last summer had been strange. Each week Frieda spent all of her allowance on romance comic books at the Busy Bee. She hid them from Shannon, told her she was too young to read them. Once when Frieda was out for the afternoon Shannon went into Frieda's bedroom. The comic books were stacked in the corner of her closet under a pair of old tennis shoes. Shannon took the top one back to her own room. She propped herself on her bed and read the whole comic. It was disappointing. There were five stories, each about some dumb girl who wanted some dumb boy to fall in love with her. In one story the girl sprained her ankle and the handsome boy came to the rescue. Another had a girl's best friend who tried to steal her boyfriend. The stories all ended happily-ever-after. Shannon couldn't understand why Frieda would rather read these silly stories than spend time with her.

Now the sun feels too hot. Shannon scoops her hair off her shoulders, lets the sweat evaporate from her neck. Her bathing suit is white with little red fish swimming across the middle and big red fish swimming around the skirt. This year Frieda has a grown-up bathing suit. It's solid green. 'The color is called 'sea-foam' ' Frieda had said.

'It shows off my figure, though I wish I had much more on top.'

'Me, too,' Shannon said, though she'd never even thought about that sort of thing. Frieda had laughed.

'You're still a child, Shannon. Such a child.'

Shannon hopes she and Frieda can be close again, like best friends. The harder she tries, though, the more distant Frieda seems. Shannon wonders why things have to change. Her parents are no help.

'You should find some friends your own age,' her mother had said. 'Don't you have anyone from your class at school you could call? Don't sit around and mope.'

So here she is, standing on the edge of the lake, squeezing the damp sand between her toes. If she stays out too long her shoulders will burn and her freckles will darken.

Freckles. There was a new boy in her class last year that she would like to call. His name is Leon but the kids called him Freckles. They called him some other names that aren't nice. He sat in the desk next to her at the back of the class, and sometimes he'd glance over at her, raise his eyebrows or make a little face as a response to something that was said. She liked his long thick eyelashes. He seemed a lot like her; shy, always watching the others. He laughed a lot, a high-pitched noise, and when he laughed he would put his hand over his mouth, as if he knew it wasn't a nice sound. The boys mimicked the sound, the covering up gesture.

One day last winter he did this amazing thing. He was sitting by himself at a corner of a table in the lunchroom, peeling a tangerine. He was taking his time, concentrating. When he finished he put the segments on his plate, and then carefully put the peeling down. He had managed to keep it all in one piece, and it looked like a whole piece of fruit, not empty at all.

'Wow,' Shannon had said. 'That's so cool.'

He held it out to her, but she wasn't sure if he meant to give it to her. It was a funny sort of offering. She shook her head and sat down at the next table. When she looked over she saw that his cheeks had turned red. She felt like she had done something wrong, but she got the feeling Leon felt the same way.

Shannon pulls the sun lounger under the big oak tree that shades most of the yard. While she waits for the sand on her feet to dry before she can brush it off, she lets herself drift in the heat. She could look up Leon's number in the phone book or get it from Directory Enquiries. There couldn't be too many Bronkowskis in the Brighton area. He got on the school bus about ten minutes after she did, in between the lakes, so maybe he could ride his bike over to the recreation area across the lake and she could meet him there. He might like to meet her at the penny arcade up by the roller rink. She has $1.50 saved up. It might be fun to play on the games with someone other than Frieda who always gets better scores than her.

On Tuesday Leon rides his bike all the way to Shannon's house. Frieda is up in her bedroom with their cousin Eve who is staying with them. Both Frieda and Eve are very nice to Leon when he arrives. They come down for some cherry Kool Aid. They pour four glasses, and cut up some apples and oranges and put them in red plastic bowls. Leon is hot after the bike ride so they drag two sun loungers down to a shady spot on the beach.

'You're so lucky to live on a lake,' he says. 'All these lakes, and I live down a little road in the middle of nowhere.

'My mom says we take the lake for granted. We've always lived here, one of the first houses on the lake. I can't imagine living in a house on a regular street. Have you got neighbors?'

'Yeah, there are kids around, but they aren't the kind I want to be friends with.'

'Why not? Don't you like any of them?'

'There's three families, lots of kids, but they're all Catholic and they stick together. They go to St Patrick's, and they talk about stuff I don't know about.'

'I know they go to catechism on Thursdays and learn about saints and things,' Shannon says.

'And they don't eat meat on Fridays. They say it would be a sin. Once, when we first moved here from Detroit, my mom asked this one boy if he'd like to have lunch with us. We had hot dogs. Then the boy's mother came over and told my mom off for giving him meat on Friday, and hadn't she thought that he might be Catholic. So mom said maybe I should just make friends at my own school. But no one there seems to like me anyway.'

'I like you,' Shannon says. 'They just need to get to know you. I'm sure they'd like you.'

Leon looks up at the sky, like he's studying the clouds.

'Have you noticed how everything comes easy to some kids? There's the ones who are good at sport. There's the smart ones. There's that kid who is always drawing.'

'And what are you good at, Leon?'

'That's the point. I'm not good at anything.' He pokes his finger in the warm sand and draws a line, and then another. 'What are you good at, Shannon?'

'I'm not good at anything either,' she says, and they both start to laugh.

'It's really not funny,' she says, but they keep laughing, and the noise carries across the water.

Frieda comes to her bedroom window.

'Hey, you two,' she calls down. 'What's so funny?'

'Nothing,' Shannon says. 'Not a thing.' But they can't stop laughing.

What She Wants
Summer 1966

'Come on, Eve. You know you want to go.'

No, Eve thought. I don't know that at all. Frieda, on the other hand, was sure. She was sure of herself and everything else. You wouldn't have thought that, at just thirteen, Frieda was a good six months younger than Eve.

What Eve wanted right now was to be left alone. She could sit at the side of this lake for hours, feeling the heat of the sun weighing down on her, burning into her forehead, and shimmering its way across the lake in a blanket of sparkles. Maybe, she thought, the most wonderful things couldn't be captured and held.

'If I tell my mom you want to go, she's sure to let us.'

Coming to stay with her cousin had been Eve's mom's idea. She'd said, 'You can spend the summer with Frieda on the lake. Aunt Barb and Uncle Rod say they'd love to have you.'

That was what she had said, Eve remembered. What she meant was, 'Then you won't be here to listen to your dad and me argue. And we won't have you as a constant reminder of why we shouldn't get a divorce.'

She'd felt safe until her brother had left home a few months back. She was afraid she wasn't enough of a reason for her family to remain a family, and now she wasn't at home to keep track of what was going on.

She scooted closer to the edge of the dock, so that the soles of her feet just settled on the surface of the water.

'Eve! Say something! Don't just sit there like an idiot. The roller rink is fun on a Friday night. Everyone says so. It's not about little kids who can't even stand up on roller skates.'

'*I* can hardly stand up on skates. Remember?'

'Well, we're not actually going to skate. I told you. It's the best place to meet guys.'

'Ask me later. Just let me sit and watch the lake for a while.'

'I don't understand you, Eve. I mean, what's the big attraction?'

Frieda stomped off in full pout. Eve poked the tips of her toes into the lake and watched as she slowly slid them under the water. She tried to soak up the stillness, find a calm place between the coolness of the water and the heat of the sun. She listened to the rhythmic lapping of the little waves against the dock and the shore, and wondered, if she concentrated hard, would they have the strength to hypnotize her thoughts?

The night she had arrived, Frieda pumped her for information about her parents' situation. Eve didn't like to think that her cousin and aunt and uncle knew there was something wrong.

'Do you hear them shouting? What do they argue about?' She had screwed up her forehead, then made her eyes huge, as she always did when she found something exciting. Eve had switched off the light so she could see the night sky from the window next to her bed, and to black out Frieda's earnest face.

'I don't know. Everything, I guess.' She didn't want to talk about it, and she resented the way Frieda could pressurize her until she said or did what her cousin wanted.

'What do you think they're doing right now? Maybe they kissed and made up.'

'Maybe. I want to go to sleep, Frieda.'

'It's not even eleven.' And then, after a moment, 'Never mind. We have the rest of the summer to talk.'

Now, less than a week later, Frieda seemed to have lost interest in Eve's parents. Good, she thought. Then she remembered how strong willed Frieda could be. Eve gave a final splash, pulled herself up from the dock, and walked up to the house. She found Frieda in her bedroom.

'Okay, Frieda,' she said. 'Tell your mom I want to go to the roller rink tomorrow night.'

It was a half-mile walk along the lakeside road to the rink. At 7.30, the sun was just setting. Frieda was heady with excitement.

'You'll probably see some of the guys from my school, but they're all nothing special.' Frieda was unbuttoning the top two buttons on her blouse as they walked along.

'Frieda, I can see your bra!'

'So—if you've got it...' She looked down at herself, and then pointedly at Eve's flat chest, and continued.

'Never mind. My mom says you're going to be a late blossomer.' Eve felt herself redden.

'I'm hoping the guys with the speedboats from the other side of the lake will be there tonight. They're staying at the campground. Some of them have cars.'

Frieda had told her about these boys a number of times.

'Stop a minute, Eve. I want to put on some lipstick and eye shadow before we get there. Where's my mirror?' She fished around the bottom of her big canvas bag. 'Remind me to wipe this off before we get home.'

'I guess we should leave by twenty to ten to walk back home in time,' Eve said.

Frieda stared intently into her little mirror as she painted blue powder from lid to brow.

'Look, Eve. Whatever happens, we'll meet back at the rink snack bar at ten to ten. We can get back home in time if we...'

'What do you mean? You're not going to desert me, are you?'

'Of course not. I mean just in case.'

The next two hours stretched before Eve. She wondered if there was something wrong with her. Was she supposed to be enjoying this evening? She looked at Frieda, tried to see her with a stranger's eyes. Somehow the make-up made her look younger, as if she were pretending to be grown up. And she hadn't outgrown her childish excitement, either. They climbed the cement steps to the roller rink complex, and Frieda bought the entry tickets.

'Two. Just the observation deck.' The bored looking man hardly glanced up.

'No skating fee, no skate rental. We'll see how far my dad's dollars will go. Come on. Let's see who's skating and who's watching.'

When Eve had come to stay with her cousin for a week last summer, skating had been Frieda's passion. Uncle Rod had driven the two of them to the rink every morning, and they stayed from 9:30 till noon. Frieda skated in a boyish, athletic way, seeing how much speed she could generate, whizzing by the less competent skaters, Eve included. Then she'd throw her head back, laughing. There was plenty to laugh at, too. Eve felt anything but secure when she had wheels clamped to her feet. She thought if she couldn't be graceful on skates, there was no point in exposing herself to the embarrassment and the bruises. And she hated being laughed at. But then, Frieda would say things like, 'You're doing really well. No one would believe you've never skated before this year. It gets easier, Eve. Look at me. A year ago I was falling all over the place.'

The skating rink did seem like another world in the evening. The thick, measured organ music that normally poured from the sound system had been replaced by a never-ending cycle of Motown tracks. Eve loved the emotions in harmony, now backed by the perpetual hum of hundreds of skate wheels on the wooden floor. And the light was different. Instead of flowing through the windows that wrapped around three walls of the rink, fluorescent light spilled from above, and the darkened windows gave Eve the feeling that life outside the rink had ceased. Everything was happening here, in this lakeside skating rink, on this Friday night.

They entered the observation deck, and before they found seats, Eve stopped to watch the forty or so skaters. They were mostly in their teens, and seemed to be a different breed than the skaters of the summer before. They flashed around at an incredible speed. Some weaved confidently; some turned and skated backwards, with the briefest of looks over their shoulders.

'Let's sit near the top,' Frieda said.

Eve turned to follow her, and saw that there were as many people watching as there were skating—maybe more. But most of them were busy chatting and calling out to each other. The people who weren't talented enough to skate were pretending to not be impressed by those who were.

'Look—there are two girls from my class. Come on. I'll introduce you.'

Frieda stopped at the end of an aisle where two pretty girls were occupied with looking bored.

'Hi, Betsy. Hi, Grace.'

The girls seemed to wake up, and focused their boredom on Frieda.

'Wow, Frieda,' one of them declared in a monotone. 'Too much blue.' She motioned to her eyes. Frieda immediately rubbed at her eye shadow with the back of her hands.

'Is that better?'

'Sure. Anyway, Grace...' the girls turned their attention away, and Frieda paused uncertainly before resuming her way up to the top row of seats. Eve looked back at them, and saw one of them mimic Frieda's eager expression, and the other roll her eyes back dramatically. They both laughed loudly. Eve was surprised by how much *she* felt the sting of this unkindness that was directed at her cousin. As they slid onto the bench she looked at Frieda, trying to read her emotions. But Frieda just said, 'They're both really popular. They could have anyone they want for a boyfriend.'

Eve wondered if you were expected to excuse hurtful behavior from the pretty and the popular. She thought of her own school. She never had a problem with the chosen few who set the standard, but this was simply because she was plain and mousey and knew her place. For all of her forwardness, Frieda obviously hadn't learned this lesson. Or, maybe she had now.

They spent a few minutes watching the skaters, and then the other observers.

'See the guy in the black shirt over there? He quit school on his sixteenth birthday. That girl who's going down the stairs is our age. Doesn't she look older?'

After a few minutes Eve stopped concentrating. She'd probably never get to know these people, and Frieda's mini-biographies all began to run together. Time limped slowly by as the skaters blurred into a haze and her mind began to wander. She thought of her own school. Her best friend had moved to Ohio in May. They had both said they'd write. Eve had received one letter. Her friend wrote that her new school was bigger than her old one, and the kids were friendly.

'You're a lovely, bright girl,' Eve's mother had said. 'Just get out there and make new friends.' She tried to imagine what her parents were doing now. She remembered Frieda's comment on that first night.

'Maybe they kissed and made up.'

Eve had thought it ridiculous—impossible. Now she let herself imagine that it might happen. Why not? They had been in love once. Perhaps her being away was a good thing.

'Earth to Eve. Come in, Eve.'

'What?' Frieda was waving a hand in front of Eve's face.

'You're such fun to be with, Eve. I'm going to the ladies room. I'll be back in a jiff.'

The thing about Frieda, Eve thought, was that she was interested in everyone and everything. And she made an effort. Eve felt hot and small. She'd been wrapped up in herself, and she'd closed poor Frieda out all week. Maybe a bit of Frieda's optimism would do her some good. Worrying certainly got her nowhere. She wondered what was taking Frieda so long. Perhaps she had run into friends. Eve looked around, trying to spot some of the people who had been pointed out earlier. She saw the girl with the wine colored top—Sandy, wasn't it?

'Everyone says she's had an abortion. And she's just a year older than us.'

Eve looked at the girl. Was it possible? When Frieda had told her, she hadn't sounded judgmental—just interested, concerned. She really was a caring person. And right now, was she saying to a friend, 'That's my cousin I'm with. She's...' what? 'She's waiting to see if her parents split up.'? 'Her best friend moved away and she's not good at making friends.'? 'She's trying not to grow up. She's afraid of everything.'? No, Frieda was too kind hearted to say those things.

'There you are, where I left you,' Frieda laughed. 'Are you bored? It must be hard when you don't know anyone. I was talking to some girls from school. They say the best place to hang out is at the new Lite-Bite. It's five minutes walk up the road.'

'But you told your dad we'd come straight to the rink, and go straight home.'

'We'll nip up there and be back in plenty of time.'

Frieda turned and headed down the steps to the exit. No chance to argue. Eve followed. She could see the red and blue neon lights of the little box restaurant on the shore of the lake. As they got closer, she saw how the lights reflected and moved on the black water. Frieda paused and looked over her shoulder.

'Good. You're coming.'

'It looks so pretty, Frieda. The lights on the lake. Don't you think?'

Frieda stopped, and took in the little light show. She turned back to Eve.

'Yeah. It does. I hadn't noticed before.' She put her arm around Eve and gave her a quick hug. Then she was pulling Eve toward the lights.

'We've only got an hour. You take the money and get the Cokes and I'll find a table out here.'

All of the leatherette booths inside the restaurant were crammed with young people. Eve bought two cokes at the counter and took them outside to the back of the building. There were even more people outside. Insects circled the outdoor lights. When they got too close they darted away again. People were laughing, shouting to be heard above the noise.

Frieda was at one of the far picnic tables, near the parking lot. As Eve edged her way around the little crowds of people, she had a bubbly, almost sick feeling in her stomach. She decided she would ignore it. Everyone was having a good time. For just one hour she would try to be like Frieda. She willed her legs to take her to the table where Frieda was waiting. There were two girls and two boys bunched together at one end. At the other, Frieda was perched on the end of the bench. A blond boy of sixteen or seventeen sat across from her. Frieda saw her coming and called to her.

'Eve! Hi! I wondered where you got to!' Frieda smiled and laughed with too much energy.

'This is Ritchie,' she nodded toward the boy. 'And his friend...'

'Alan. I'm Alan.' Eve noticed a short boy who stood a yard or so behind Ritchie.

'They've come from the camp ground on their motorbikes. That's them, over there.'

Ritchie seemed to visibly puff up as the bikes received appreciative glances from the girls. Eve put the Cokes on the picnic table. Frieda didn't seem to notice. Ritchie fixed his gaze on Frieda.

'So, anyway, it makes a noise, but it's a smooth ride. Come on. I'll take you to the campground and back. You'll love it.'

'Well...' Frieda looked as though she had already made up her mind to go.

'Frieda!' Eve pointed to her watch.

'I'll have her back in twenty minutes, little mother. You could go with Alan,' both Eve and Alan avoided eye contact with the others, 'or Alan, you could lend Frieda your crash helmet and stay here with...That would be best, don't you think?'

'Have my Coke, Alan. I haven't touched it.' Frieda turned to Eve. 'I'll meet you here by a quarter to...' and she whispered harshly into Eve's ear '*Talk* to Alan.'

Eve watched as they climbed onto the bike. Alan's helmet looked huge on Frieda's head. She waved to Eve, and anyone else who might notice, and wrapped her arms around this new friend. Eve watched as the motorbike roared out of the parking lot. She sank onto the bench, and closed her eyes to block everything out. 'Frieda will be okay,' she told herself. 'She'll be back in half an hour. She won't want her dad to be angry. She'll want to come out again next Friday.'

'He's an okay guy, you know,' Alan was sitting across from her now. 'Really. Don't worry. You look so scared. He'll have her back. . .' He toyed with the straw in Frieda's drink.

Eve couldn't think of a thing to say to Alan. He sat quietly across the table. The minutes crawled by. She was looking at her watch at a quarter to ten, when Ritchie's motorbike pulled into the parking lot. Frieda wasn't on the back.

'Where is she?'

'She's coming back with some guy in a Mustang. She obviously likes them better than motorbikes.' Eve could hear the anger in Ritchie's voice. She was angry now, too.

'Let's go, Alan,' Ritchie said.

'Do you want me to stay until she gets back?' Alan asked Eve.

'She said she was a big girl, and would be on her way back in a few minutes. She told me to tell you, Eve.'

Eve nodded so that they would go.

'Bye,' Alan said, and followed Ritchie back to the bikes.

When Frieda hadn't arrived back by ten, Eve suddenly thought, 'Of course! I've got it wrong. They will have driven the other way around the lake. She'll be back at the skating rink, waiting for me.'

There weren't so many people at the Lite-Bite now. She picked up her bag and started running to the skating rink. The street lamps cast circles of lights under them, and she rushed from each one to the next, afraid of what might be hiding in the dark. Then she felt too exposed in the lamplight. She could see that the lights at the roller rink were being turned off, section by section. Just one remained on outside as she reached the building. There were a few people milling around, waiting for rides, or talking. A girl of eighteen or so walked up to her.

'Are you okay?'

She found she was crying.

'My cousin. She was supposed to meet me here. She went off...'

A car pulled up in front of the roller rink. Eve felt a rush of relief. Then she realized it was her Uncle Rod.

'Eve? Where's Frieda?'

Eve tried to explain about the Lite-Bite, and Ritchie and the motorbike—and the Mustang. She couldn't stop crying. Her uncle drove to the restaurant, and then the campgrounds. He was angry and scared, and shouting as if Frieda was in the car with them. It was after eleven when they drove up to the house. Aunt Barb came out, and when she saw that Frieda wasn't in the car she covered her mouth and said, 'No, no.'

When the police came, Eve explained what had happened. They asked her a lot of questions. She described Ritchie for them, and tried to think if he had said anything about the Mustang or its owner. They said she must try to remember, what kind of motorcycle was it?

'I'm sorry. I don't know. He said it was a really smooth ride. Does that help?' Aunt Barb was crying again.

One of the policemen said, 'It's gone one o'clock. We'd better let this girl get to bed.' To Eve he said, 'Your cousin will most likely turn up by the morning.'

She pulled herself to her feet, and walked to the bedroom, at first relieved to leave, and then frightened to be left alone with her thoughts. She slipped out of her clothes, then into her pajamas. She thought she'd toss and turn all night, but the past few hours had left her exhausted. She looked out of the window. Was that the same sky of just a week ago? She closed her eyes and fell asleep.

She opened them again to the thin grey light of early morning. She thought she had been dreaming of her father. His voice seemed to linger in her ears. Then she realized she was hearing voices from some other part of the house. She looked over to see if Frieda was awake, and saw the undisturbed bed. The previous night came back to her in a rush. She got up and walked to the bedroom door, and out into the hall, listening. She heard her father's voice again.

She came to the kitchen door. Her dad, mom, and Uncle Rod sat silently hunched over coffee cups at the table. She wanted to go to her mom, but delayed for just a moment, not wanting them to confirm what she already knew. Frieda had not returned.

Her mother turned around, as if she had sensed Eve's presence. She rose, and went to Eve. She brought her back, sat her in the chair where she had been sitting, and ran her hand up and down Eve's back.

'She isn't home, Uncle Rod?' Eve asked in a voice just louder than a whisper.

'No...Not yet.' He tried to smile as he spoke.

'Where's Aunt Barb?'

'She's having a little rest. Waiting is hard,' her mom said, and then leaned over, kissed her on the top of the head, and sat down in the chair next to her. It was the chair where Frieda sat to eat her meals. Uncle Rod stood up.

'I'll just go check on Barb.'

As he left the room, Eve's dad placed his hand over hers.

'We thank God you're alright,' he said. She didn't know what to say.

'Eve,' her mom said, 'we've talked to your Aunt Barb and Uncle Rod, and the police said it's okay for Dad to take you home later this morning.'

'Just Dad?'

'Well, yes. I'm going to stay. Barb needs her big sister right now. You go back with your dad. I'll be home soon.'

'Can't I stay until Frieda gets back?'

Eve watched her parents exchange a look.

'I'm not sure how to explain this, Eve,' her mom started.

'I understand, Mom. We don't know were Frieda is now. But I want to stay, to be here. I want us all to be together.'

Her dad took a deep breath and sighed. Then he said, 'Eve, I promise the three of us will all be home together soon. It's what we all want.'

She looked from her dad to her mom, who nodded, and whispered, 'Yes.' For a moment Eve could hear Frieda's voice in her head. *Maybe they kissed and made up.*

'The thing is. . .' Her father's words brought her back. 'The thing is, Aunt Barbara might find it hard for you to be here right now, without Frieda. Can you understand?'

Eve's mom continued, 'Let's wait and see how Barb is coping. We'll decide later this morning. Right now though, why don't you try to get another couple of hours sleep? It's not even six. Would you do that, Eve? It would be the best thing.'

'Okay. You'll wake me if anything...'

'Yes, of course,' her dad said.

The idea of going back to bed was good. It felt as if Eve had been given permission to not worry for a while. She walked quietly down the hall, past Frieda's parents' closed bedroom door, past Shannon's bedroom, and back to Frieda's room. She crawled back into the bed under the window. The sun was starting to burn the grey from the sky now. It would be hot later on. She turned her head toward Frieda's bed. It seemed to her, if she tried really hard, she should be able to sense if her cousin was okay.

She got up and took Frieda's bathrobe from the hook on the back of the door. She slipped her arms into it. As she wrapped it tightly around her she breathed in the sweet citrus of Frieda's spray cologne. She pushed her hands deep into the empty pockets. She felt so tired. She pulled back the sheet on her cousin's bed, slid in, and fell asleep.

Sally Ann Why
Summer 1966

Dear Diary,

Summer stretches. Nothing happens. Then, when something finally does happen no one will talk to me about it. Someone who I know, who actually lives on this lake, has disappeared. Mom calls her that poor girl. Did I know that poor girl? What was that poor girl like? I said of course. She sat next to me on the school bus sometimes. And her name is Frieda, not that poor girl. When I asked where she might have gone Mom clammed up. I said she probably just ran away because she wasn't popular at school. Mom said her parents were destroyed. That was her word. Destroyed. I asked if she would be destroyed if I ran away from home. Not that I ever would. She looked shocked, like she'd been punched in the stomach, but she said I would never do that. I'm sensible. Subject closed.

I had more questions. For instance, why was her father up at the Busy Bee buying beer and cold cuts just a few days after his daughter goes missing? He didn't look destroyed. He looked normal. And why did that girl's friend leave her at the roller rink to come home alone? And why has Mom started hiding the newspapers from me?

Diary, Howard is so much cooler than the boys my age. They are all first class morons at school. They need to GROW UP. Howard, on the other hand, has a deep voice. I've heard him shouting at other kids. And he slicks his hair back like a hood. Mom says keep away from the hoods, but they are the most exciting thing around here. I know his house is kind of falling apart, but he can't help that. At least he doesn't have parents who want everything to be NICE all the time. He goes to the junior high school where they have all kinds of clubs and stuff to do. When I go I'm going to join the young writer's club and, if I'm really brave, the drama club. I'll put my imagination to good use, and some people around here will see that they are just trying to hold me back. And I won't be like Howard's brother George who wants to be in the band, so he can do exactly what he's told or what the music says he should do. George doesn't like it when I ask him questions about Howard. Everyone keeps secrets or doesn't want to tell me stuff. Why should anyone have to grow up in a place like this?

It's exciting to know that, when I'm sitting on a sun lounger on the beach Howard might walk by at any moment. I've checked. It takes three hundred and twenty-three steps to walk from our property to his. That means right now he's less than three hundred and fifty steps away. I wonder if he is asleep yet, but he's probably watching TV or something. I'm sure *he* doesn't have to go to bed before ten on a weeknight. (I wonder if he writes in a diary under the covers using a flashlight. It makes the whole thing more exciting, like I'm writing mysteries.) The last time he walked over my property I didn't say a word. I just stared at him and he stared at me. I felt so stupid, but I didn't see him coming, and then there he was, sloshing through the water ankle deep. Next time, diary, I'll say something—and something better than 'Hi.' Next time I'll get it right.

Love,
SA

Mae Meek
Summer 1966

At dawn, the lake is at its calmest, the water is still a blanket of night. By turns it looks solid, then thick liquid, maybe the consistency of tar. And then, as the sun almost reaches over the tops of the trees, you would think you could dip your hand in and it would come out dripping black. The birds are waking, intent on defending their territories. The people in the houses, the early risers, don't hear the urgency of the birdsong. The troubles of others are never as bleak as your own. The birds sound happy enough to Mae.

She has been awake for hours, playing the past week's news over and over in her mind. That poor girl, Frieda. Mae had been shocked when she'd seen the picture on the local news. She knew the girl, had spoken to her a couple of times. The newscaster had said 'disappeared,' putting so much emphasis on the word, you knew you were supposed to wonder about all the possible horrors the girl would have experienced. Mae wonders if she is living some horror at this moment. She wonders if Frieda is still alive.

Shame washes over her. She knows this feeling. She first felt it when her daughter Justine died almost twenty years ago. Mae had been sixty-three. She had been stunned, so devastated by emotions she didn't think she would survive. But she had survived, and that is where the shame came in. She had told her husband Sal, no mother should outlive her child. It wasn't just a thought. She felt it to her core.

Now, this girl. Mae has watched her growing up on the lake. She keeps remembering one time two summers ago at Marv's bakery when she'd dropped her change purse. Coins rolled away in different directions. Mae couldn't bend down, not with her back problem. The girl had hunted down every coin and handed them back to her. Mae had said something like, 'Oh, thank you. Let me buy you a bun or a doughnut.' The girl's eyes had widened, but she'd said, 'No, no. You don't need to do that,' and she'd smiled and bounced out the door. Mae remembers this clearly. And now, Mae is almost eighty-three, and the child's life may be over. Mae can't imagine otherwise, though she tries. She can't imagine that shining girl just running away.

Mae turns her attention to her aching back. She can picture her spine, bones grinding, crumbling, creating fine dust, giving her a hunched look. She's seen women younger than herself with that dowager's hump. She's sure she doesn't look *that* bad. She eats sensibly and has kept her weight down. She doesn't even need to bother with her glasses since the cataract operation.

The sun has cleared the treetops. She makes herself a strong cup of coffee, looks out at the lake from her dining room window. Mondays are her favorite day of the week. Her next-door neighbors Hector and Blanche take her out on the lake on Mondays, late afternoon. Mae will have to fill her day until then.

At ten o'clock there are a few boats on the lake. The black water has turned to dark blue. The surface looks stippled, a constantly changing un-pattern. Wavelets lap on sand that is more yellow-grey than gold. It's going to be hot today. Some wise people are making use of the cooler temperature, doing jobs that would melt them later in the day. The first lawn mowers hum from over and around, a pleasant buzz, a summery voice. Somewhere a duck squawks its single note over and again. Another joins in angry conversation. This lake has been Mae's life for more than thirty years. She, Sal and Justine used to come camping here, when there were no more than a dozen houses dotted around. They lived in the sweltering city heat all week, then headed out on Friday nights in the Hudson for two days and two nights of tented bliss. Then they'd bought the house on the hill. It was a fixer-upper when they moved in and, because of Sal's first heart attack soon after the move, it had stayed a fixer-upper. They were lucky to sell it and move into this lovely little box cottage. The hill house stood empty during the winters for some years. And summer people didn't want to spend their time working on the house. For the past eight or ten years it has belonged to Betty with all the kids. Mae has watched its decline. She wonders how it is still standing; all rotten wood and boarded-up windows. It must be so cold in the winter.

At one, children splash and squeal in cool water as the sun sits almost directly overhead. Mothers set picnic tables for lunch, sandwiches, chips, sodas and beer under huge umbrellas, understated blues and greens or splashes of color you could see from way out on the lake. Someone clang-clangs a bell calling the kids home from their adventures to a family meal, gobbled quickly so the mandatory hour before swimming again can start ticking away. The afternoon stretches like the whole summer. This could be another planet from the winter one, or the city one. Inboard motors, outboard motors sing the joy of it. Mae feels a little rush of glad-to-be-alive. She wonders what her life would have been like if they had stayed in the city. She sips iced tea and peels herself an apple, the green skin a long spiral. She slices little manageable chunks, stops to inhale the pale scent as she brings the first piece to her mouth. Her sense of smell has faded, the sweet-tart apple only hints at flavor. Once again she pushes loss from her mind, but finds she's settling back to thinking of Sal. Sal was the driving force in the family, the person in charge.

One day he had said, 'Mae, we have got to move further out from the city. One or two negro families in the neighborhood is one thing, but if we wait much longer, we'll be surrounded by them. And they don't like us any more than we like them.' Mae hated it when Sal talked that way, assuming she agreed with whatever he said.

When they saw the for sale sign in the little yard of the hill house, though, she agreed. He had been due to retire in a year. He would have been able to drive in, or stay with his brother if the travelling turned out too much.

Now, she looks around the lake, and is sad that there still isn't one brown face to be seen. She wonders why the two cultures are so separate. Is it shame covered over with anger? There are marches in the south. She's seen them on TV, angry faces, the great-great grandchildren of slaves, no doubt, wanting to be treated the same as all the white people. It sounds reasonable to Mae. Sal didn't live long enough to see this. She can imagine how he would have reacted. She used to hold her tongue when he talked. Now she finds she answers the TV back. 'Oh, for heaven's sake. They're people, too.' She imagines Sal shaking his head at her, 'Mae, Mae, Mae...,' his barely masked exasperation, as if he were talking to a silly child. She pushes this ugly memory of her Sal away, and goes to have a little nap among the cushions on her sofa. She'll float a while, listen to the breeze rustle the elms and the oak. She'll push everything else out of her mind for a bit, and be at her best for the boat ride.

At four, Mae is sitting on her porch. The house is locked up, and she has her key in the deep pocket of her dress. Her wide-rimmed straw hat, the one she has had for twenty years, sits in her lap, and she waits for her invitation. She can see that Hector's pontoon boat is ready, the cushy chairs all pointing forward, the cooler, full of bottles of Blanche's lovely lemonade no doubt. Hector walks from his house to hers and offers, 'Are we ready to go, ma'am?' with the usual slight bow. He loops his arm through hers until they get to her half dozen steps down to the beach. He takes her elbow and steadies her across the sand and along his dock. Then Blanche reaches out from the boat and helps her over the little gangway. Mae feels as if she is precious cargo. She ties the ribbon of her hat snugly under her chin, and slides into one of the orange life preservers, her fingers fiddling a bit over the metal clasps. There is another couple on the boat, friends visiting Hector and Blanche from Alabama. Once Mae is settled, Blanche introduces them, but her voice is too fine for Mae to quite catch every word. Is the man called Clayton? The woman's name seems to have been snatched away by the breeze, but it doesn't matter. She can hear the men's voices well enough. She likes listening to Clayton's slow, gracious-sounding lilt. And Hector's booming New England accent is plenty loud enough for her. She feels that lovely slight swell of excitement stretch through her rib cage as the big pontoon's motor hums.

'Jackets all on?' Hector asks. Then, 'Full speed ahead.' This is Hector's usual little joke. The boat glides slowly out about thirty feet from the shore and starts its long, leisurely circle of the lake, counter clockwise, with Hector's grand house at 12 o'clock, of course. Then past Mae's, and the dozen or so cottages like it, each modest and functional with a short stretch of grass and twenty or so feet of beach. They suit her idea of good, temperate lives. Being on the lake is what elevates them to extraordinary.

They are getting close to the Blue Lantern and the public beach, and the houses grow more luxurious. There are a few that seem to well up from their front yards, looking disapprovingly down at the lake, and all the inferior houses.

The Blue Lantern has certainly been through changes over the years. It still has a mystical quality when it is lit up on summer weekend evenings with its dance band music humming across the water. Hector takes them quite close so they can see the white side of the building that protrudes straight from the water. The constant slap of waves has left a line of green slime, not very glamorous at all. Mae has never been inside, so her imagination pictures what it might be like. She sees a large wooden dance floor, a platform for the band, maybe a few red cushioned chairs, nothing too fancy, scattered in clumps here and there. She remembers some dance hall from when she was a young girl, but can't quite place it.

She's aware of a braying laugh, loud enough to startle her out of reminiscing. It's Clayton's other half. Mae smiles politely at everyone and turns back to watching the shoreline. They seem to be happy to leave her alone.

Hector skirts the boat away from the public beach, giving the swimmers a wide berth. He comes close to the big island.

'That's where the bodies are buried,' he crows. Blanche flashes him a look of disgust, and Hector starts to explain to the visitors about Frieda, the girl who has gone missing.

'I wasn't thinking of that when I said...what I said.' He seems to want to change the subject, but Clayton's Mrs. is leaning forward asking questions, something about possibilities, then suspects.

'Well, people are talking. There's a couple of "possibilities' as you say,' but Hector drops his voice, and his face has a confidential look to it. He's pointing toward a house back in their area of the lake. Then he spins back around and gestures towards her old house on the hill at the edge of the lagoon.

'I'll show you when we get there,' he says. 'Oh, listen to that. A train is coming.' Soon Mae can pick up the long two-toned wail of a freight train. Hector is pointing to the little corner of the lake where the train will appear, and sure enough, an impossibly long freight train slides through the gap. Everyone smiles their approval and watches until the caboose slips out of sight, and the wail slides away with it. Hector steers for the entrance of the lagoon.

'The boat's too big to take you in. Some years, when the lake is high we can get her in, but the mosquito population is pretty rife in there anyway.' He slows to a stop, and they all look over the scrubby bushes along the sand barrier.

In the quiet of the lagoon a girl carefully rows in the afternoon heat, among the lily pads, waxy yellow flowers like balls of warm butter, and white flowers, scattered like stars on their green sky. Weeds grow thick there. They stop only when they brush their sky. They wave and sway like mermaid hair, as if they are trying to work themselves free of the murky water. But where would they go? The girl is a solitary child. Mae thinks of Justine out on the lake, imagines herself as a child. Perhaps this girl doesn't like to run off the end of the dock, doesn't like to splash in the chest-deep water. Perhaps she doesn't like to play, or maybe she just doesn't fit. They aren't close enough to tell how old she is, but she appears skinny and awkward. It looks like she's wearing a life belt. She pushes the oar handles down low so the tips are high in the air. She is so still, and when she does move, she seems to do so in slow motion. Mae starts to shudder. She hugs her arms around herself, hoping no one will notice.

Hector has started up the motor again, and takes them as close as he can to the hill house. Whenever they pass it, Blanche and Hector comment on what a disgrace it is. Mae hears Blanche say, 'a real eyesore,' and Mae is glad she has never told them that she used to live there. She thinks they seem to enjoy tutting over it a bit too much.

Hector is talking about a teenage boy who lives there, and Blanche says, 'No, Hector. He's just a kid.' Then Hector says, 'Is that a police car parked behind the house? I think it is. Maybe we should just carry on, or we'll start looking like the suspicious ones.'

Damn, Mae thinks. Damn damn damn. Now she hates the fact that she can only catch bits of conversations. She's not sure why Hector would suspect one of the boys from the hill house, isn't sure what he is suspecting him of. She adjusts her back against the chair cushion. Blanche is offering her lemonade or a can of soda pop. Blanche always offers, even though Mae never accepts out on the lake. They are nice people really, Mae chides herself. She settles back to enjoy the rest of the ride. The motor hums and everyone seems lost in their own thoughts. Hector points out the head of a turtle about twenty or thirty feet from the boat, but Mae's eyes can't focus well enough to see it. Then she hears, 'at that house there. Muskrats. A whole family of them.' Mae wonders what a muskrat looks like. She has no idea, but she smiles to herself at the thought of sharing the lake with this wildlife. She closes her eyes for a minute. Why does she feel so tired?

'There,' she hears Hector say. 'What did I tell you? He's always looking through those binoculars. If that isn't suspicious I don't know what is.' She can just see the man, sitting on a little seawall. He appears to be focusing on them all in the boat, but he might be looking past them.

'If he lived on a smaller lake, he wouldn't need those binoculars,' Clayton says. Mae sighs. Why do people feel the need to talk about things they don't know about? And what could be worse than not knowing?

As they glide along past families sitting at picnic tables, an older couple, a baby under the umbrella of its stroller, children holding hands and running into the lake, assorted people on lawn chairs, others lying on towels on the beach, Mae wonders what it would feel like to unfasten her life preserver, get up and open the little gate at the side of the boat, to let herself slip gently into the deep blue water. She feels sure she wouldn't float for more than a second or two. She can almost feel the pressure of the water, feel it pulling her down.

Property
Late Summer 1966

Suddenly she doesn't belong to us. And it's not just that she's gone, and I won't let myself think where she's gone if I can stop myself. It's like she isn't our property anymore, her mother and me. And of course I don't mean property, but she belonged to us, she was part of this family and now this family is falling apart.

What I mean by doesn't belong is this: she's in the papers, she's on the local news. I don't know where they got that photograph of her laughing because every time I tried to take her picture she'd wrinkle her nose and put her head down like she was ashamed or something.

Property. The police asked us to identify the things they found in the campgrounds. Her wallet, that little bottle of her mother's perfume that went missing two months ago, and that strange postcard with the young couple on it. I don't know if that was hers. I'd never seen it before, didn't even recognize the writing on it. It wasn't English, and she just speaks English, but it's the kind of thing she would like. They didn't find her handbag, but they found the little pink compact that her mother gave her last Christmas. I remember thinking no, she's too young for that. Barb said, 'She'll love it. Just watch her face when she opens it.' Pink plastic, beige powder. And a lipstick called Tangee Natural that she must have bought for herself. It looked like orange wax. I smelled the lipstick tube. It was sweet and sharp, and I remember Frieda smelling like that sometimes when she left the house. They showed us all the things for us to confirm they were hers, but then they wouldn't let us have them. 'Evidence' they said. Evidence of what, I can't bear to think.

People cross the street to avoid me. Sometimes it makes me mad and other times it's a relief not to have to talk, to hold it all together for someone who can't begin to imagine what we're going through. A few come over to say how sorry they are. Someone who I don't even know came up to me in the Busy Bee and said, 'I'm sorry for your loss.' I wanted to say she's not lost. Don't say she's lost. We just don't know, and the not knowing is the hardest. I was looking for the lipstick, the Tangee Natural. I don't know why, but I just wanted to have it, to be able to smell it. I couldn't find any, but they had masses of those romance comics that Frieda spent so much money on. Every Friday when she'd get her allowance she'd be up at the Busy Bee buying one. I could imagine her standing in the magazine section, making her choice.

I remember when she was a little girl she was always openly watching, always trying to figure people out. It was as if she was working out how to fit. I would watch her watching. I thought she was beautiful and innocent. If you could have seen her eyes: so blue, so curious, as if she could eat the world up by just looking at it. She was a bit bossy with her little sister, but she never tried to be the centre of attention. She wasn't loud. She didn't cry much. I can't remember the last time I saw her cry. When I think of how frightened she must have been it takes my breath away. I wonder if she cried. Did she think of me, wonder why I wasn't there to rescue her? Did she think of me at all?

That woman who came to the door, I didn't know her from Adam, and she said, 'I'm praying for your daughter.' I stood there. I started to cry, a grown man sobbing. I don't remember what I said to the woman. I like to think of the woman, praying for Frieda. I like to think there's a God up there to hear. I can find a sliver of comfort in that.

Barb can't. She says the woman was nuts and should have stayed away. She's more angry than me most of the time. That's a big problem, too. We're never in the same place with our feelings, and it takes too much energy to try to understand each other. We used to be able to practically see into each other's minds. That's how close we were. Who would have thought there could be anything that would pull us apart?

I know I should be the strong one. I should be able to muster up some anger, and I should be there for Barb, but I just feel broken.

Last night I had a nightmare. I have lots of them, but they seem to dissolve when I wake up. I'm sure that's a good thing. But this one was different. The house was dark, and there was a noise at the door. It wasn't a knock. It was more like a scraping and a rustling. I felt like I was pulling myself awake. I walked down the stairs, and it took ages to walk down. The stairs went on and on, and the front hall stretched such a long way. I was afraid to open the door, but I knew I had to. When I opened it there was this horrible huge bird, bigger than me. It was black, like a giant crow, or maybe a raven. It spread its wings out and stood there. It had this horrible grey beak that took up most of its face, and there was blood in its eyes. It opened its beak and threw its head back and it laughed. But the most terrible thing was it had a man's laugh, like something from a horror movie. It laughed and laughed until I could pull myself from the nightmare. I sat up in bed, and I could hear my wife Barb. She was crying in her sleep, sort of whimpering. I thought I should wake her, save her from whatever horror she was going through, but I left her alone in the bed. I walked downstairs.

It was reassuring that the stairs were normal again. I went through the kitchen to the back door, and out to the back yard. The grass was long and wet. I haven't mowed it in more than a month and I forgot to put my slippers on. I walked over to the hammock. I would have usually brought it in to the garage by this time of year. I stretched out on it and looked up to the stars. They were so bright. I tried to imagine Frieda somewhere. She might be looking up at the stars. The very same stars. You don't know. It's little things like that that help me to be able to carry on, day to day. I stayed until dawn started to fade the stars, and I went back to bed. I felt kind of damp from being outdoors. Autumn is almost here, and that's a horrible thought. But I crawled into bed next to Barb. She was sleeping peacefully.

In the morning I didn't tell her about the dream. What's the point?

On the Edge
Early Autumn 1966

It's hot. Too hot. Vincent had set his alarm clock to give himself an extra ten minutes. Now he wishes he hadn't. Soon he'll have to go to the school bus stop and wait with the other kids, all hyped up for the first day of school.

He doesn't want to let go of the lake. He's up to his knees in it, edging into it. He wishes he'd spent more time drawing the lake weed. He should have opened his eyes under water and watched the way it looked, suspended, swaying. Sometimes it grows until it reaches the surface. Then it looks like a rug thrown out over a part of the lake. He should have drawn that. And the dead weed washed up on the shoreline. He can smell the tang of decay, that fishy smell. He never drew the dead fish either, like the one here, dead-eye staring, flies buzzing. How do you get that down on paper?

'Vincent,' his mom calls. 'You're going to be late.'

He sloshes out of the water and into the house where he quickly slips into his school pants, puts his school things in his blue canvas bag. He gets to the stop as the yellow bus turns onto the top of his road. He sits at a window near the front. He sees Howard and two of his brothers running toward the bus as they are pulling away. The driver eases back to a stop.

'We're not going to start this again, are we, boys?' the driver says. 'You don't need to make everyone late.'

The boys say nothing. Vincent concentrates on looking out the window. He feels Howard slide onto the seat next to him.

'Hello, buddy boy.'

'Hi, Howard.'

Howard is in a good mood. He's talking and joking with some of the older kids. Good, Vincent thinks. He'll leave me alone. But the bus has another four stops, and a half hour is a long time. After a few minutes he starts.

'So, Spanky. First day at junior high. Are you nervous? Are you scared? All those big fish, and you, a scrappy little minnow?'

Vincent feels his throat tighten. He tries to think of something to say, but so many thoughts are buzzing and he can't get a hold of anything safe. He can feel sweat prickling under his arms. He has been watching Howard's foot on his blue bag, pushing it under the seat in front of him leaving dusty footprints on it. Howard sees that he's noticed, and gives him a wide-eyed innocent look. The bus is taking forever to get into Brighton. Vincent wonders if every day is going to be like this. He has his art class to look forward to later in the week, but other than that, school will be torture.

'Hey, Squirt. How's about you let me sit by the window?'

Howard stands up and Vincent scoots out of the seat. He feels Howard's hard knuckled jab to his shoulder. He wonders if anyone has seen, if they would say anything if they had. The bus driver growls 'sit down, you kids.' For the rest of the journey Howard looks out the window. When they pull up to the junior high school Vincent reaches over to see if he can get to his book bag. Howard stretches out his leg to stop his effort. As the bus stops, a girl in the window seat ahead turns, kneeling on her seat. She hands Vincent his bag, then shoots Howard an angry look.

'Why do you have to be so mean?' she asks.

Howard looks surprised. The girl is Vincent's age, but they had different teachers at the elementary school. He thinks he remembers she's called Sandy, or Sally. Howard mimics the girl's voice under his breath. Vincent collects his bag from her and says thanks. They head into the big front entrance together.

Sally Ann—Beginnings
Early Autumn 1966

Dear Diary,

My first week in Jr. High and I've learned a lot. It's so different from grade school. You go to a classroom, you have your class, then a bell rings and everyone spills out into the halls and charges to their next class. You get five minutes to get there and get settled. Fifty-five minutes later you change again. Up and down the stairs, back and forth. People are calling out to each other. The cool kids are busy being cool and the greasers are busy trying to look mean and moody. The rest of us are trying hard not to trip or drop our books or run into a wall. (I saw that happen to a rather large girl. Oh, the humiliation. But no one laughed.)

I had a nightmare last night. I almost missed the school bus. I couldn't find my locker, and when I did I couldn't remember the combination for my lock. Then I realized I didn't have my books, and I couldn't remember what my first class was or where my classroom was. I looked down to see if I was still in my pyjamas, or, worse yet, was stark naked (I've had that dream before) but I was wearing a pink ball gown, which was apparently okay. When I woke up I was afraid to go back to sleep in case my brain invented some new horrors to torture myself.

School: my English teacher is lovely. She just started teaching, and she's bursting with enthusiasm. I know her class is going to be great. American History is okay. Math is okay. Science is okay.

And the school bus: what surprised me most was that no one said a word about Frieda. I thought they would all talk about nothing else. Has she just been forgotten? Since she disappeared Mom has been impossible. I can't walk to the Busy Bee, can't take the rowboat out alone. She keeps the doors locked. I asked her why. What was she afraid of? What did she think happened to Frieda? She said it's not for me to worry about. Whenever she says don't worry I know I should worry. At church Reverend Edison still says we should pray for her. There were some ladies talking about her in the community hall after a service last month. One of them said the word RAPE. I asked Mom what that was, but she changed the subject. She used to talk to me about things because I'm the oldest. Now I just get DON'T WORRY. I guess she thinks she's worrying enough for all of us. I tried looking that word up in the dictionary, but it didn't make any sense.

And Howard: what did I ever see in that boy? He's just mean and nasty. I used to think he was so cute. Now I can see that he's ugly.

But, dear diary, I have made a friend, and he's a boy. His name is Vincent.

Love,
SA

A Nice Life
Early Autumn 1966

Vincent couldn't help being envious. All around Island Lake there were families. There were the ones who lived in the big houses. They had big docks. They had big boats with big inboard motors, or the sluggish pontoon boats that floated around grandly, as if they were little chunks of land.

The littler houses packed in collections: sisters, brothers, cousins, friends. There were badminton nets stretched across lawns, sun loungers, folding chairs, picnic tables, swing sets. The hotel had two big swing sets, two slides, a teeter-totter, and one of those things that you pushed around in a circle and then jumped on. There were still people swimming in the lake, playing in the sand, even now, late in September. You could hear their voices, carried over the water.

In the late afternoon you would catch the whiff of barbeques. Sometimes you would hear people laughing or singing, or calling out, 'Okay, hon, bring the burgers. The fire is ready...just right...time for the marshmallows...be careful not to burn your mouth.' Vincent's mom cooked their burgers in the house on the stove. No marshmallows.

Everywhere, there were family and friends. The 4th of July had been the worst. The lake was crammed with boats, so many voices, so many people having so much fun. You could smell hotdogs and hamburgers and steaks and ribs. At about 10.30 at night the drive-in movie in town started their annual firework display. Vincent couldn't see them from his vantage point on the lake, but could hear the boom-boom-boom as they went off. Out of reach; all the good stuff was out of reach.

On Saturday morning Vincent's mom went into town to get groceries. He usually went with her to help carry the bags, but this morning when she came to his bedroom door at 10 o'clock he pretended to be asleep. He was letting his mind wander to see where it would go, but he didn't like where it was taking him. A bit later she came back.

'Vincent, I'm going to get groceries. Don't stay in bed all morning.'

Once she was gone he got up and poured a bowl of cereal and turned on the TV. He flipped between channels: cartoons, an old *Lone Ranger* episode, *Milky's Party Time*. They all seemed silly and pointless. On the half hour *Fury-the-Story-of-a-Horse-and-the-Boy-Who-Loved-Him* came on. It was the episode where the horse was going to die. Everyone was sure of it because Fury had lain down and wouldn't get up again. Joey, the boy, slept next to him in the barn all night. He talked to the horse, reminded him of all the good times and great scrapes they had survived together. Joey cried a bit. Vincent found he was close to tears, too. His throat hurt. He wanted to cry like a little boy. But then Fury pulled himself to his feet and whinnied, and everyone was happy. Joey had a horse and a dad, or was he adopted? Vincent couldn't remember the early episodes. The man loved him the way a dad should. Every week was a happily-ever-after. Real life wasn't like that.

He turned off the TV and pulled on his clothes. He got his art stuff from his closet and spread a few things on the table so his mom wouldn't think he'd wasted the morning. He was waiting for enthusiasm to arrive when he heard the car drive up. He went out to help his mom carry in the bags.

'Well, Vincent, you'll never guess. I met a nice man at the meat counter. We were both waiting for them to put out more ground chuck and we got to talking. He's renting a house right here on the lake. He says he doesn't know a soul here. So later this afternoon I'm going to meet him at the Little Skipper Inn for coffee.'

'What's his name?'

'Roy.'

Vincent's mom hadn't been out with a man since his dad left. He guessed he should be happy for her. He tried to be.

'Enjoy your date,' he said as she was leaving later in the afternoon.

'It's not a date. It's...just coffee.' She'd taken over an hour to get ready for just coffee. She'd put on makeup, washed it off and then put it on again. And she'd tried on lots of clothes, arranged them on the bed, then decided on white slacks and a navy blue top.

'I'll be home by seven to make dinner,' she said. 'Are you going to draw some pictures while I'm gone? Maybe you should go out in the yard and get some fresh air while you can. The weather is supposed to turn chilly later next week.'

'Okay. Sure,' he said, but he didn't plan to leave the house. He locked the door after her.

What he wanted to do was phone his dad. Vincent hadn't phoned him in three weeks, and it seemed long enough for his dad not to be annoyed. He wouldn't tell him about his mom going out with the man. He didn't think his dad would be interested. He waited a half hour before he called. He let it ring twelve times before he gave up. He watched some college football on TV, and then tried again. This time it rang twenty times before he slammed the receiver down. He didn't know why it made him so angry. He told himself he didn't give a fig about his dad and his new family.

His mom got home at 7.20. She said Roy was coming for a barbeque the next evening, 'to catch the last of the good weather.'

The next afternoon they dragged Dad's old barbeque out of the garage. Vincent's mom dusted off the cobwebs and tried to shine it up a bit. She set it on the lawn where his dad used to put it. She found a full bag of charcoal and a can of lighter fluid.

'Do you think we should try to start it, or wait for Roy to get here?' She sounded nervous and excited.

'We?' Vincent said. 'I don't know how. Dad never let me near it. Remember? I guess you should wait for the man to come.' His voice sounded more angry than he had meant it to. He didn't know why. Maybe he'd like this Roy. Maybe this Roy would make his mom happy. He hated the way she usually folded in on herself. He told himself he should be happy.

'Vincent, you're going to be nice to Roy, aren't you? He'll be our guest. I don't want him to see this sullen behavior.'

She went back in the house to finish making the potato salad. Vincent poured charcoal into the big metal bowl of the barbeque and put the grill rack back in place. He went in the house.

'You want me to chop some tomatoes and cucumber?' he asked.

'Thanks, sweetie.'

Roy arrived at exactly 5 o'clock. He brought a six-pack of beer and a brown paper bag.

'Thought I'd bring dessert—make a contribution. I brought Neapolitan ice cream. I wanted to bring spumoni or tutti-frutti, but the Italian grocery in the city is closed on a Sunday. And everybody loves Neapolitan.' Vincent thought Roy sounded just as nervous as his mom. He was surprised. He thought grown-ups would have everything figured out.

'Goodness, you've gone to a lot of trouble,' she said. 'The problem is we only have a tiny freezer section, and it's already full.'

'What a disaster,' Roy laughed. 'I'll tell you what. Do you have an old newspaper?'

He took the two ice cube trays from the freezer, put one under and one on top of the carton. Then he wrapped it tightly in the newspaper and shoved it in the back corner of the refrigerator.

'That should keep it frozen for a few hours. Do you want a beer?' He pulled two bottles from the six-pack. Vincent had never seen his mom drink beer. She got the bottle opener from the drawer and took two glasses down from the cupboard.

'I'll have mine o-naturale, if you don't mind. Less to wash.'

It was strange watching these two grownups. Vincent wondered if his mother would drink from the bottle. She wouldn't even drink Coke from a bottle, always insisted Vincent use a glass. 'So much more civilized' she would always say, though now she quietly put one glass away, poured beer in the other. Vincent got up and took the glass back out and got the iced tea from the refrigerator.

'Oh, sorry, hon,' she said to Vincent.

'It's okay,' Vincent said. He took his drink outside on the porch. He didn't like feeling like a fifth wheel in his own house, and they where both so nervous they made him feel uncomfortable.

He thought about the girl he'd met on the school bus last week. Sally Ann. She was nice, and she was funny. She had a brother and two sisters, or maybe it was two brothers and a sister. They were all younger than her.

'You don't know how lucky you are to be an only child,' she'd said. 'I feel like I get lost in the crowd at my house. I never get any peace.'

There was something odd about Sally Ann, something a little too eager, like she was buzzing with too much energy. Maybe all girls were like that. Vincent thought she would make a good friend. He wondered if, now that he was in junior high school, boys and girls could be friends. You never saw boys and girls together unless they were boyfriend and girlfriend. He didn't like the idea of having a girlfriend. He wondered if Sally Ann thought about him. If she did she probably thought there was something odd about him. That made him laugh.

'First sign of madness, laughing to yourself.' Roy had come to light the barbeque. He was carrying a tray with hot dogs and hamburgers on it. 'You want to help?' he said.

'I'll just watch.'

'Pour some more charcoal on for me, will you? There isn't enough on here to roast a mosquito.'

The bag was heavy. Too many poured out at once.

'Whoa! Whoa!' Roy laughed. They both started picking up lumps of charcoal and putting them back in the bag.

'That's good,' Roy said. He looked at his hands, black with charcoal. Vincent walked down to the shore and scooped up a handful of wet sand. He rubbed his hands together and rinsed them at the water's edge. They were a pale grey.

'Needs soap,' he said, and went into the house. Roy followed, and they both walked to the bathroom. Vincent's mom came to see what was happening.

'Just a mishap with the charcoal,' Roy said. Vincent thought he sounded sheepish.

'Well, see that you boys don't get my towels dirty.'

It sounded funny, "you boys", and both Roy and Vincent giggled a bit.

'To tell you the truth,' Roy said, 'I've never done a barbeque in my life.'

'Me neither.'

'Don't tell your mom. Maybe she won't notice we're a couple of amateurs.'

There wasn't much lighter fluid in the can, and Roy squirted it all in the middle. It took a while, but they got the fire going. Vincent had the feeling his mom was inside watching, letting them get on with it. Once the charcoals had been stirred around and the hamburgers got going she started bringing out the salad and buns. She set the picnic table with dishes.

'Looks like we're out of paper plates,' she said. They never used paper plates. Vincent wondered why his mother was trying to be someone she wasn't. Was it so important to have a boyfriend or girlfriend that you pretended to be what you think they wanted? His dad had never done that.

Dinner worked out fine. Vincent's mom said she liked the hamburger, even though it was burned a little. Roy seemed to enjoy his potato salad an awful lot. He had a couple more beers. It started to get breezy. Roy said if they had used paper plates they would be chasing them down the beach. They all helped carry everything back in the house.

Roy insisted that he and Vincent do the dishes. It was only when they were half done that they remembered the ice cream.

'Forget drying,' Roy told Vincent. 'You dish out the ice cream. We can leave these to drain dry.'

Vincent unwrapped the carton. It opened like a treasure box so you could see the three colors, the vanilla, chocolate and strawberry. It was soft around the edges. Vincent took the back of a spoon and slowly started swirling the colors together. He watched how the brown of the chocolate was stronger than the pink and creamy white. He scraped the tip of the spoon along the edges of the pink and white, making a pale chalky color. Then he realized that Roy was talking. He thought he had said the name Howard.

'Hey. What are you doing, boy? We don't all want to eat slop. Just dish it out.' He didn't sound too angry, though.

'What were you saying?' Vincent said.

'I was asking if you had friends around the lake. Do you kids get together?'

'You asked about Howard. Mom said you didn't know anyone. Why were you asking about him if you don't know anyone?'

Roy didn't say anything for a minute.

'I just used to sort of know him,' he said. 'Do you know where he lives?'

Roy was staring at him, a hard look that Vincent didn't understand. He took the spoon he had been working with and plunged it into the ice cream. He walked to his bedroom and closed the door.

'Vincent?' his mother called. Then, 'Vincent! Come out here. Come and tell me what's going on.'

'Ask your friend. Ask him what he's doing here.'

Vincent had never told his mother about Howard, how the boy took pleasure in hurting him. He didn't like to upset her. That was part of it. But in some weird way he felt like not telling her was a way of punishing her.

After a while he heard the front door close. His mom came to his door and knocked quietly and then walked in. Vincent was under the covers, though he hadn't changed into his PJ'S. She sat on the edge of the bed next to him.

'Tell me about Howard,' she said.

'No.'

'Please, Vincent. I want to know what's going on.'

'No. I have to go through this alone because you're so weak and Dad's not here.'

He knew he was hurting her. He knew she would be starting to cry, silently and wordlessly. It didn't make him feel any better.

'Howard is a bully. He makes me feel stupid and small.' He looked up at his mother. 'He scares me. Why does that man want to know about him?'

'Because 'that man'...Roy...is his father.'

For a few minutes no one spoke. Then Vincent's mom got up and walked to the door.

'Don't worry, Vincent.' Her voice sounded choked. 'He won't be coming here again.'

Watching Robert Duffin
Early Autumn 1966

'You're not going to die. Your mother's not going to die. I'm not going to die. At least not any time soon. Now stop worrying, turn off the television and go and do something constructive. Worrying is not constructive.'

My parents never let me watch the news. They say there is no point. Mom says I take things too much to heart; I'm just too sensitive. Dad says I have morbid curiosity; I dwell on horror. They say the news has nothing to do with me. What do I care if there is an earthquake in Turkey, a flood in China? These things are far away, and no amount of feeling bad can help the people involved. And knowing a lot of details is just sick.

Mom says childhood should be a happy time. When I was little, and used to dream about the bombers coming, I'd call out in my sleep. I'd see my bedroom in flames, bricks and rubble scattered everywhere. Mom would take me into her bed, telling me to keep quiet so I wouldn't wake Dad. Once, when I started crying and woke him, he said to Mom, 'What now?'

Mom explained that I'd had a nightmare about the house being bombed. He said to me, 'Don't you worry, Ruth. John Wayne will come and save you.' And then he said to Mom, 'No more war movies for her.' He turned over and was snoring in about two minutes.

Four years ago, when I was eight, we had the Cuban missile crisis. It was really scary. Everyone was talking about it. The boys in my class said the Russians were sure to bomb us all. They said they were going to join the Army as soon as they were eighteen, and would save the U.S.A., and all of us girls, if there was anyone alive left to save. They didn't sound scared at all. They sounded really excited, and spent a lot of time acting out battles in the playground.

I did a sort of survey. I asked every teacher I knew if there was going to be a war. Almost all of them said things like 'I hope not,' or 'Whatever happens I'm sure we'll be safe here in Brighton.' Mr Franks, the gym teacher said, 'It doesn't look good.' Only Mr Talcott, the sixth grade teacher, said, 'No. It will all blow over. You'll see.'

And when it did, I decided that he was the smartest man I knew. When he would see me in the hall after that he used to wink at me. Even now, when I see someone wink, I feel like they must have some special knowledge to make them feel so confident about things.

Now the Vietnam War is a different thing all together. It's about Communism, but I don't understand much more than that.

When I visit Grandma we watch the news, and she lets me read the newspapers. I wish I understood how it started, and why young men go to the other side of the world to fight. Grandma says the military teaches you to hate, so it makes it easier to fight and kill. She says it's necessary, to keep the world safe from Communism.

Up until a month ago, talking to Grandma was as close as I'd come to the war in Vietnam. Then something really terrible happened.

There's a boy who lives across the street from us. His name is Robert Duffin. I didn't notice him until two years ago, when he was sixteen, and got his first car. It was old and very noisy. I started watching him from my bedroom window. He parked the car in the driveway, and was always washing and polishing it. Then he painted red and yellow flames along the sides. I thought it looked amazing. When my dad saw it he laughed and laughed. He started calling him 'Hot Rod'—not so that Robert heard him. We live in the kind of neighbourhood where no one but the kids get to know each other. The grown-ups keep themselves to themselves.

Robert had lots of friends, boys and girls. People were always dropping by at his house when his parents and mine were at work. And they had lots of barbecues and parties in their back yard all summer.

That all stopped about the time I went back to school after summer vacation. I didn't see Robert or his friends for a couple of months. Then I saw him in an Army uniform. He was home for about a week, and all his old friends came to see him in their cars. Dad had stopped calling him 'Hot Rod,' and he didn't mutter about the noise of the cars, either.

When Robert went away again the street returned to being peaceful. Two months ago I overheard Mom talking on the phone to Aunt Toni. She said she had heard that our neighbour's son had been hurt in Vietnam –'injured badly' she said. I started imagining all sorts of horrible things, like him being burned, and having no hair or eyebrows, or paralysed, in a wheelchair. He wouldn't be able to get up the steps to his house.

Then he came home. I saw his parent's car drive up, and watched him get out of the back seat. He wasn't wearing a uniform any more. He had a little bandage on his forehead, and one covering his hand, but other than that he looked fine.

His mother stayed home from work for a few days, to look after him, I guess. Some of his friends came to visit in their cars, but none of them stayed for very long.

When he had been home for just over a week and I had stopped thinking about him so much, Donald Hopper stopped me in the hall at school.

'Hey, Ruth. Don't you live on the same street as Robert Duffin?'

'Yes. He lives across the street from me. He's home from Vietnam. He was injured, but he's better now.'

'Better? How do you get better from having your hand blown off?'

Donald Hopper is one of those boys that tells you something to shock you, and then likes to see the look on your face. I don't remember saying anything to him after that. I was just seeing Robert Duffin in my mind, getting out of his dad's car, or standing at his front door waving goodbye to one of his friends, not even stepping out onto the porch.

When I got home from school I got a book, an apple, and a kitchen chair, and went out and sat on my front porch. I was pretending to read the book, but I just kept reading the same paragraph over and over. What I was really doing was watching for Robert. I was trying to work out if it was his left or right hand that was gone. I didn't see him at all that day.

The next day I did the same thing. Robert's car had been backed out of the garage, and was sitting in the driveway. After a while he came out, and went to sit in his car. I was there with my apple and my book. I was trying to read the book only using one hand. That meant I had to put it down in my lap to take a bite of my apple. Then I put the apple down on the floor next to the chair, and my book slid out of my lap. I picked it up and tried to open it with just one hand. I looked across the street to Robert in his car. I could tell by the way his head was tilted that he was watching me in his rear view mirror. He got out of his car and walked to the curb. He called to me in a really nasty voice.

'You want to come over and get a really good look?'

I could feel my face, just burning. I got up and walked slowly toward him. I had to apologize, to tell him I just felt bad for him. I told myself I wouldn't look where the bandage was. I wouldn't let myself, no matter what. I was standing just a few feet in front of him. His eyes were so angry I couldn't bear to look at them, either. Then I heard a car horn, and kind of felt a car coming towards me. Robert reached out with both arms, and yanked me by my sweater right out of the road. The car swerved around where I had been standing.

'Are you crazy?' he shouted, but he didn't sound angry—he sounded scared.

I said, 'I'm sorry.' I think I said it a couple of times. Then I was looking at the bandage. My brain kept saying, 'look at his face,' but I couldn't stop myself. My eyes kept going back to his hand, or where his hand used to be. There was a silence - the kind that feels so big, because everyone thinks there are no words good enough to fill the emptiness. I heard myself say, 'Does it hurt?'

'Yeah, it hurts. It hurts like hell. It feels like my whole hand hurts—every finger—every fingernail. And they're not even there. How can that be?'

He looked at me, as if I really might have the answer. What could I say? I'm just a kid—a stupid ignorant kid. I don't know anything.

'I don't know. It isn't fair. It just isn't fair.'

'That's how I feel. Why me? Everyone acts like, "Oh well, bad luck. It just happened." *I* wasn't any less brave, any less careful than anyone else. It just isn't fair.'

He started to cry—big loud scary sobs. I'd never heard anyone cry with a man's voice. They never cried in the movies. I stroked his arm, near the elbow, where I thought it wouldn't hurt. Then I took him by the hand and walked him up the steps and into his house. I steered him to the couch and he sat down. He was taking big gulps of air, like he was trying hard to get in control. I went to the kitchen and got a glass, went to the fridge and took the milk out. I decided it would seem more normal if both of us had a drink, so I got another glass and poured us milk. I carried them into the living room where Robert was blowing his nose. He wiped his eyes on his sleeve, and took one of the glasses from me.

We didn't talk while we drank. He drank his more slowly than me, and when he finished he said, 'Thanks. Want to watch some T.V.?'

I nodded, and we settled down to watch. We sat together like two old friends, watching while Tom and Jerry smashed each other to smithereens.

At the Breakfast Table
Autumn 1966

It was hot for mid October. Just when Vincent was getting used to the idea of autumn and winter this Indian summer Saturday arrived. By mid afternoon a nasty smell began wafting around the lake. People started closing their windows, phoning the authorities. Vincent had wanted to sit outside on a lawn chair and watch the sun and the clouds behind the flaming trees, but the smell caught in the back of his throat. It made him feel sick, so he went inside and leafed his way through his scrapbook, the pictures he'd done in the summer.

The peach Howard had so deliberately placed had seeped through the first three pages. He'd started afresh after that, colors and designs, fanciful groups of people and animals, stripes and more squares, fish and more fish. He hadn't looked at the drawings since school had started, and now he tried to get back to the feeling he'd had early in the summer.

The smell outside was leaking into the house. The phone rang and his mother answered it. He went into his bedroom and closed the door. He could still hear his mother's voice, catch phrases, 'that family' and 'septic tank.' His mother's laugh was high and sweet sounding. He didn't hear that sound very often. When his father left he took most of the joy from her life, and Vincent had no idea how to put it back.

The smell seemed to be soaking into his room, into his curtains and the quilt on his bed. He could almost picture it, like a grey-brown fog. His mother tapped on his door.

'Come on, Vincent. We're going into Brighton for an early dinner. Maybe the smell will be gone by the time we get home. I'll tell you all about it in the car.'

*

On Monday Howard and his brothers weren't on the school bus. Stories of the septic tank floated around the bus, at first quietly, conspiratorially. Vincent thought he must not have been the only victim of those boys. By Wednesday everyone knew that Howard and his family had been evicted from the house. No one knew where they had gone. Some of the older girls speculated that the family might have been broken up. The smell of the clogged septic tank had invited in the authorities. There was no working stove. One of the upstairs windows had fallen out and an old mattress was propped against the hole. Vincent kept hearing the words 'unfit mother.' That was the kindest thing they said.

On Friday Sally Ann joined Vincent on the morning ride in. The topic of conversation on the bus had moved on. Now the older kids were talking about the Halloween dance coming up next week.

'Have you noticed,' Sally Ann said in a quiet voice a few inches from his ear, 'how much they talked about that family, and no one has mentioned Frieda?' Vincent rested his forehead on the window and let the vibrations bump him for a minute.

'I don't know,' he said. 'I don't understand people at all.'

He had always been careful not to talk about Howard to anyone. Not even Sally Ann. He was sure it would only make matters worse. He thought about Howard, how nasty he'd been, but wondering about him wouldn't help anything. He didn't want to think about him any more. But he'd hardly thought about Frieda at all. What kind of person did that make him? He had a hard time getting to sleep that night.

Vincent was awakened by a sound at his window. He lay in bed for a minute, trying to work out if he had dreamed the little raspy sound. Then he heard someone whisper his name. He peeked through the edge of his venetian blind. Sally Ann stood, lightly scratching the screen window.

'Vincent. Get dressed and come with me.'

It was just past sunrise. Vincent pulled on his jeans and a sweatshirt. He tiptoed through the house and silently opened the side door. Sally Ann was waiting. He put a finger to his lips to shush her until they were away from the house. They walked down to the lake. The air hung wetly over the still water.

'Where are we going?'

'Howard's house.'

Vincent stopped.

'It's all right. There's no one there. Don't you want to see what it's like?'

They started walking on the damp sand at the water's edge, quietly. Vincent wanted to feel bad for Howard, but every time he tried he felt anger in his chest like a small powerful fire.

There was no beach in front of Howard's house. They had to pick their way among rocks and overgrown grass. There was a padlock on the door and an official-looking notice pasted above the metal mailbox.

'Come on,' Sally coaxed. 'We can look in the window.'

Vincent followed her, but he didn't want to. He'd never been inside the house though he had wondered about it, all those kids.

The curtains were pushed back at one window at the side of the house. They climbed over some ragged bushes until they were against the wall. They cupped their hands around their eyes to block out the weak sun that fell over their shoulders.

The authorities must have come while they were having breakfast. Bowls and glasses looked to be scattered across a wooden table that took up most of the room. There was a big box of cornflakes and a bottle of milk spilled out on the table, and half a dozen big gray rats were feasting on what was left. Vincent stepped back and lost his footing. He fell into one of the bushes. He could feel a sob trying to make its way up his throat. He didn't understand why. Sally let him pull himself to his feet.

They walked back to his house without a word. She stood a few feet from him and gave a little wave, then turned and continued on to her own home. He watches her round shoulders, her head down. He let himself in the side door and went to his bedroom. He undressed and slipped back into his pajamas. He felt desperately tired, but he knew if he closed his eyes he'd see the breakfast table and the gray rats. He stared up at the ceiling.

Self Expression
Autumn 1966

It's not as if he ever sat me down and said this to me. And you have to understand, this is in no way a criticism, but what my father taught me is this: there is no problem so big that you can't run away from it.

Leave that for a minute. The thing that my mother taught me: everything hurts if you let it.

Now, I can understand both, I guess, and I've got to say, neither sounds that appealing. So I figure I stand somewhere in the middle. They'll both think I'm wrong whatever I do.

My life seems to be a string of things that just happen. I lie in bed at night trying to think what I can do to make everyone see things the way I see them. For the past week I've been working on this plan. I never really thought I'd get a chance, but it seems like this was meant to happen.

Vincent used to imagine he could stop his mother crying. He would just have to get out of his bed and walk through the dark hall to find her alone in her bedroom or at the kitchen table. He would say the right things to make everything all right. He would drift off to sleep thinking what he would do. But in the morning he would find her in the kitchen, tired and puffy-eyed. And he could never remember the point at which he let go of her pain and found his own comfort in sleep. She seemed to find a solution herself in the end—of sorts. She blocked everything out and made herself numb, distant. Anyway, she doesn't cry much anymore.

Vincent quietly closes the art room door behind him, although he knows there is no one around to hear. Sometimes circumstance seems to invite a solution. Every student, every teacher is in the school assembly hall, waiting for the principal to make some announcement. Vincent is sure he won't be missed, and now he is ready to put his plan to work. He pushes the wooden tables and plastic chairs away from the center of the room, ready to start.

He empties the waste-paper basket on the floor, but quickly realizes that this isn't right. Other people's discarded paper, the brown apple core, and the sticky ball of used scotch tape don't fit his plan. He carefully collects it up and puts the bin back in the corner of the room. He takes paper, fresh, clean, white paper from the cupboard. He runs his finger over the little lock as he closes the door. Would someone get in trouble for not locking the cupboard? No. His mind flashes an image of what the room will soon look like. No one will worry about a cupboard.

He picks up a thick wedge of paper and cradles it in his left arm. He pulls away a pile an inch or so thick, and lets it slide from his right hand. Most of the paper falls quickly, weighing itself down. But the last few slip more slowly, and flutter and swirl to the floor. He drops paper again and again. With another two armfuls a pile has begun to grow. Vincent walks around the edge of his circle. Any sheets of paper that have strayed too far from the jagged formation are picked up and wadded, bunched into loose balls. He stops to study a sheet as he crumples it, random fold upon fold, complicated and unique. The little pockets of air, the oxygen, would be fuel.

'See, you did learn something useful in those science classes,' he half sneers. He knows how things work well enough. He doesn't see the point of learning laws and theories, understanding patterns. School leaves him cold. There is nothing he can do with science or math. It nails him down, keeps him from moving. English isn't much better, with more rules - grammar, punctuation, all getting in the way of what he feels. And the literature. Mrs Brandt starts picking at a story before they get halfway into the plot.

'See this... Notice how the author... What is he telling us here?'

Vincent can't concentrate. Sometimes he can't keep up. Other times they expect him to slow down. It's frustrating. The point of every piece is lost to him when it's taken apart, dissected, like the poor lifeless lamb's heart his biology teacher prodded, smiling with enthusiasm.

'And this, boys, is the left ventricle. Notice how it joins...'

Vincent tosses a last wad of paper to join the twenty or so in the center of his mound and goes back to the cupboard, to the drawer where the paints are kept. He reaches in with both hands and picks up as many tubes as he can. His hands are sweaty with excitement, not fear, and he has trouble unscrewing the first top. He squirts most of the contents over the paper. A small red squiggle is almost lost on the disordered mound. He opens two more tubes, and with both hands squeezes them together, so that their contents mingle along the edge of the paper.

He tosses the empty tubes to the centre of the circle, works his way methodically around the paper, returning three times with more tubes. He pauses briefly a few times to watch the colors as they merge and intensify on the white background. Then he catches sight of the big bottles of poster paint on the counter by the sink, a dozen or so bottles in six colors. So limiting. Frustrating.

'We'll be working with pencil this semester. Then we'll progress to poster paint. Don't think you can rush at Art. Don't be in a hurry. And don't bother trying to express your feelings. They are irrelevant at this point. You need to learn the basics. You need structure. Otherwise your attempts will be useless. I don't care what you did at elementary school. Now I want you to learn properly, from scratch.'

Elementary school had been great. Miss Beavis was so kind and encouraging. She said nice things to all the children, true. But one day, shortly after Dad had moved out, she stood and watched Vincent while he worked with some stubby bits of colored chalk.

'Tell me about what you are drawing, Vincent.'

People didn't usually ask him what he thought or felt. They just told him what they saw. He can't remember now what he'd said, something about trying to get everything on paper, so he could hold onto it, so it wouldn't change.

'You can come use the art room whenever you need to, Vincent. Just make sure that I know you're here.'

That had helped. It was good to get his feelings on paper. And although the pictures didn't always make sense, he would try to explain them to Miss Beavis. She didn't say the pictures were nice or pretty and she didn't say she understood things when she didn't. Once she told him 'Your work is quite exceptional.' He turned the phrase over again and again in his mind, until the statement became concrete to him. He had one person who understood him, or at least thought it was worth trying.

Some months later, one of his Saturdays with his dad, they drove to Detroit together.

'What will it be, Vincent? Belle Isle? The zoo? Your choice, son.'

'What I'd like most of all is to go to the Institute of Arts.'

'What for?' His dad furrowed his forehead and looked down his nose at him.

'They have an exhibit of abstract expressionism. It's supposed to be amazing. Mrs Beavis told me about it.'

'You're kidding, right? No? Okay, it's you're call. But you'll have to explain things. Modern art just looks like things gone crazy to me. If you can make any sense of it I'll be glad to hear it.'

They climbed the wide stairs into the building and entered a large empty hall. There were a number of huge murals, paintings of the inside of a car factory. They took up the whole of two walls, and they made Vincent gasp out loud.

'Looks a lot nicer than the one your old man works in every night.'

The first room of the exhibition held about a dozen huge canvases; each seeming to have a personality of its own. Vincent knew he would need to study each in turn, and block everything out while he did. He heard his dad muttering under his breath. He was looking from canvas to canvas, shaking his head. Vincent thought that maybe he could explain what he saw, how it made him feel. Maybe he could make his dad understand his excitement. He tried, but he couldn't find the right words. And he was wasting the little time he had, trying.

'Look, sunshine. How about you look on your own. You'll be safe as long as you stay in the museum. I'll go get a coffee and read my newspaper. I'll come find you at lunchtime and we'll go get a burger. Is that okay with you?'

Two hours. Vincent wanted to see everything, not miss a thing. But seeing everything would mean not spending much time on anything. And there were the sculptures, three-dimensional art. He'd never seen anything like them before. It was all he could do to keep his hands off the pieces. Everything needed time, to be figured out, and maybe understood. In the end he just forgot about time and drifted from piece to piece as if he was consuming snatches from a huge feast. He couldn't get over the shapes and images, some obvious, some hidden, like puzzles teasing him, making his mind work hard. And the artists used so many different materials: metals, wood, mirrors, acrylic, paper...

Paper. Vincent has lost track of time. How long has he been standing, remembering? That day had been the beginning of the end of his relationship with his dad. They weren't alike at all. They just made each other feel uncomfortable. Now, less than a year later, they never went anywhere together. And last week his dad hadn't even remembered his birthday. No present, not even a phone call. But that day at the Detroit Institute of Arts, his dad didn't even realize the gift he was giving. And now Vincent knows he can bide his time, and wait for more days, more discoveries.

He reaches into his pocket and takes out a book of matches. It sits in his hand, a startling yellow. He tosses the unopened matches into the centre where it perches amongst the flattened metal tubes. He imagines his mound on the polished floor of one of the rooms at the Art Institute, with people slowly circling it, trying to understand. He sees his mom looking vague and aloof, his dad confused and distracted. And his art teacher? Well, he'd soon get his chance!

Vincent leaves the room and quickly walks to the boys' lavatory, where he closes himself in a cubicle, waiting for the assembly to finish. Emotions swirl and bubble like storm clouds. He feels a bit of guilt and shame, but easily pushes those feelings aside. As his art teacher has instructed, he concentrates on the now. He smiles to himself, imagining what will happen next.

The Streets of Boston: Interview
Autumn 1995

In his occasional series 'Street Life' our reporter Tim Graves interviews another interesting stranger on the streets of Boston.

I first encountered Howard B. at the Orange Line Downtown Crossing station in August. I was running late for a meeting in Back Bay. I could feel the heat intensify as I headed down the stairs and made my way to an empty bench. I passed a busker, a craggy guy with a guitar that had seen better days. His strumming was pretty basic, and his voice something between a rasp and a shout. He was singing the same line over and over, 'Everybody's Eddie's friend, everybody's Eddie's friend.' I remember being annoyed. The train was taking too long and the busker was monotonous. I watched a few people dropping change or dollar bills into his hat, more than I would have expected, considering the calibre of the talent. He stopped singing at one point and laughingly requested a hundred dollar bill from a finely dressed woman. She laughed, too, as if they were both in on a joke. I heard someone say, 'Hey, How!' Someone else said, 'Are you taking requests today?' And there were a few comments about Eddie. 'Tell Eddie I said hi.' Then he started singing again, 'Everybody's Eddie's friend.'

There was something in the heat and the buzz of the station, and the hypnotic bluesy pull of the song. I could feel myself being drawn in. I settled back to enjoy the entertainment. When the train came I found I was reluctant to leave. I felt I'd been witness to something special— something that happens once in a blue moon—a bit of magic. I was also rather ashamed that I hadn't dropped so much as a red cent into his hat.

I looked out for him, tried going to the station at the same time, then at random times, but I didn't see him again. Then, early in October I got off the T on the northbound side, and I could hear him, singing about Eddie. I raced down and over to his side of the station, flashed my Charlie card at the barrier, and went to sit next to him. I listened to him sing. A train came and went, and I listened some more. When the second train came and went he turned to me and said, 'Don't you have a home to go to?' I put some folded bills into his hat. He took them out and put them in his pocket.

'Don't want people to think I'm doing too well,' he said. I asked him if I could buy him dinner. He suggested I come back in an hour. I was obviously biting into the most lucrative time of his day.

I spent the time at a coffee shop, jotting down questions I wanted to ask the man. An hour later I went back to the station. He was waiting for me. We headed for a little Italian restaurant in the North End. I asked if he minded if I asked him questions.

'Look,' he said. 'When I eat, I eat. If you want to talk we can go to a bar after. I'll buy the drinks.'

I told him that wouldn't be necessary, but he insisted. That was his part of the deal. He was very appreciative; we made polite conversation as we ate, about the food, about the magazine. He thanked me a number of times, and he enjoyed every mouthful.

Later, at an Irish bar, he bought us both a beer and I took out my list of questions. I needn't have bothered. I asked him one question and he talked for an hour with little prompting, as if his story had been brewing for years, waiting to be told. I asked, 'So, who is Eddie?'

'He's nobody and he's anybody, the person you wish you knew, or wished you were. We all want to be Eddie, the guy who gets it right, the guy you look forward to seeing and you know you'll miss when he walks out the door. I'd give anything to be Eddie. Wouldn't you? But no one can teach you how, and your life is just a bundle of choices. Have you noticed how one bad choice can lead to another, and then another? Before you know it you've made a mess of your life and you have no idea how to undo. You can't undo. So you start blaming everybody else, like if you can pass the misery on to them you can feel better about yourself. It's like scoring a little victory for team 'you.'

'I've lost a lot of people along the way, and I'm sorry. I grew up a long way from here, oldest kid of six. I haven't seen any of my brothers or sisters in, oh, thirty years. I wonder how they all turned out. It wasn't until it was too late that I learned: to get something good you had to put in something good.'

I asked him where he grew up.

'There's this place in Michigan, somewhere near Detroit and Ann Arbor, that has a lot of lakes, like God or some giant sprinkled them all over the place. I lived on one of those lakes in the important years, seven to fifteen. When I dream I always go back to that lake. It was beautiful, but I was too angry about my life to see it at the time. I was the oldest, so I thought that gave me certain rights. I don't think I was really bad, but I was a bully. I'm ashamed of that. But then something bad happened and people started blaming me. Then the authorities got involved, stuck their noses in, and took my family apart. I never really had a dad, and they said my mom was unfit. They scattered us kids in foster families and children's homes. And no one wanted a rotten egg like Howard.'

I wanted to know more about the "bad thing" that had happened to maybe put his life into context. Howard has a way of staring off while he collects his thoughts. Sometimes he answers a question straight off, and sometimes it feels like he has to do a lot of searching to find the right words. When I asked, he batted the question away, just said 'someone disappeared.'

'Were you involved in any way?' I asked.

There was a flash of anger in his eyes, and he looked hard at me and said, 'No way, no way, no way. I was just a kid. I was just a kid, but people started talking, listing the bad stuff I'd done—just mischief, you know. And the girl lived close by. Some people put two and two together, and they imagined, and they liked a nice juicy story.'

I began to wonder if Howard was putting me into that category, so I changed the subject.

'So, when did you leave Michigan? And how did you come to end up in Boston?'

'The draft took me out of Michigan, and Vietnam taught me a lot of ugly things and left me with some bad habits. The years after I got back were pretty much a blur. I had no reason to go back to Michigan. I had a friend from Nam who came home to Boston, so I came along with him. But once we got back he fell into his old life and I wasn't a part of it. Then, it's an old story. I mixed with the wrong crowd, didn't make the right choices. There's whole years that I couldn't tell you what I did, how I got by. When I turned forty I decided to get clean and make something of myself. It wouldn't seem a lot by some people's standards, but I held some regular jobs, got some of my teeth fixed, got this beautiful smile.' He laughed, showing one gold front tooth and a few gaps.

'When I got laid off five years ago, I wasn't going to find another job. Not at my age. I could have felt sorry for myself, could have gone under. But I thought I'd give busking a try.'

'Tell me about your music, Howard.'

He roared with laughter.

'I don't pretend I'm something I'm not. I'm just a guy who sings on the subway to make enough to get by. Boston's a great city, and a lot of people are kind. That came as a surprise to me. You can sing to Harvard professors and you can sing to Joe Soap. Sometimes the poor people are generous. I like that. A dime from a poor man is like $25.00 from a rich guy. I don't think anyone will ever give me $25.00. I know my voice isn't worth it, and I'm not even that musical anyways. I had a brother who was musical. I've lost track of him. I've lost track.'

As always, I gave my subject the opportunity to make a statement or give advice to our readers. When I told Howard this was how I would close the article, he laughed long and hard.

'Look,' he said, 'I'm forty-nine years old and I busk for a living. You want me to give advice? Okay. Here goes. Stay clean. Stay sincere. Hold on to those who are close to you. The worst thing in life is loneliness. I know.'

Girl Without Skin
Spring 2005

I found the notebook last week in a little recess in the wall in the basement. By this time we'd lived in the house for years. The basement had never been finished off, and we thought it would make a nice playroom for the kids.

I was doing some preliminary work before my builder friend was going to start, and I saw what I thought looked like a little book peeking out from behind a joist. It's rusty red and it looks like it has been there awhile. The first few pages are numbers, like adding up bills. Boring stuff. I was going to throw it out, but for some reason I flicked through it. At the back of the book I found the pages, written in pencil. I sat down and read it. I've got to tell you, it made me feel sick to my stomach. I showed my wife and she was reading it and saying, 'Oh my God, Hal. Oh my god.' In the middle of the book was the page of doodles, with her name in the middle and all these daisies growing out of it. Frieda. There were just six pages with her writing, and the page of doodles. Daisies and faces, and a little Santa Claus, for Christ's sake.

We sat with it at the kitchen table, drinking coffee and trying to get our heads around what it meant. My wife knew the story of a girl that went missing out on one of the lakes near Brighton back in the sixties. She said her mother told her to scare her into not coming home late, not going off with strangers. She told her when she was the same age as Frieda was when she went missing. My wife said it didn't really sink in, didn't make her behave any better, but she remembered the name.

We thought maybe it might be a hoax, but it wasn't put there to be found, that I know for sure. I went into town and took a copy of those pages before I gave it to the police. Don't ask me why I did that. I knew what would happen once the police had it. I'd hear nothing. But I felt like it belonged to the house. The house where me, my wife and two kids have lived for years. Our babies were born here, for Christ's sake.

The police said they knew the case, and that the girl's sister had received a letter from Frieda back in 1968. Or maybe it was a birthday card, but they said they knew the girl wasn't murdered. The envelope was franked in San Francisco. I don't know. I've got a lot of questions and no one to answer them. If it happened today there'd be all kinds of stuff on the Internet. And umpteen families have lived in this house since...

My wife says it's hard to sleep in this house since we read the notebook. I've got to say, I don't like the idea of my kids being here. We want to sell up and move, but once the police come and tear up the basement, who's going to buy it? I think of that girl in the basement. I keep thinking about her, alone down there. I try not to think about when she wasn't alone.

Listening to the chatterbox voices in my head.

When he's gone
and all the locks are
locked
and the quiet drives me
crazy
I tune in.

I start by singing
songs to myself
loud
motown and Liverpool
christmas carols
old doowap dad sings
when he forgets himself.

I try to catch his voice in my head.
Come on Frieda. Let's go let's go let's go
and HOWDY, PARTNER
his John Wayne voice
and mom humming
a lullaby she used to sing to me
and used to sing to Shannon
and now she's too old to be rocked to sleep
and I rock myself to sleep here.

Eve.
Unsure and afraid
faltering words
I should have been afraid
Should have listened

Hiss and chirp—summer bugs—brush the sand off my feet
—to walk to the busy bee—up the hill—edge the road—then
cut through to Grand River—bees and hornets—dragon flies
from the lake—careful weaving—up the path—hand in pocket
—a dollar bill and some change—buy a love comic—mostly
pictures—few words—to float my mind away

I'm a fish in an aquarium
a rabbit in a box
I used up all the oxygen
a long time ago
I used to know kindness
I'll never know it again
Fish caught hooked captured
de-scaled and gutted—dead and alive
Rabbit strangled and skinned
No rabbit foot luck—dead and alive

dead and alive
dead and alive
dead and alive
dead and alive
dead and alive

Nice things: The girl on the bus that always smiled at me.
The songs in church, the songs at Christmas. Sunshine
springtime dancing class fireworks and sparklers
grandma's rocking horse in the garage, Shannon laughing
at my silly jokes, roasting marshmallows

Sweet things: Roasting marshmallows, my favorite
ornaments for the Christmas tree, china bells that really
tinkle, one legged Santa, swimming under water, the motor
boat ride, Hush-a-bye, Jergens hand lotion, pink bottle bubble
bath, my room, my home

Places: My room, my home, the tree in the back yard—maple,
the big tree in front of grandma's house, the drive in movie,
the lake the dock the sand the islands, the tiny little island
next to the big island, the lagoon, the busy bee, the bakery,
little skippers inn, school, the gym decorated for a dance,
carnation wrist corsages, trampoline

When I Disappeared

I imagine my mother cried
for days and nights and days and more.
My father would have been angry
thick with rage, fists and pumping veins.

And what about the girls at school?
Did they find nice things to say about me
when they saw my face on the local news?

Some of my teachers probably had to stop and think.
Had they even noticed the plain girl
who never said a word but smiled
hoping a smile would be enough?

I am not a filthy girl. I can't do this any more